MR. (ALMOST) RIGHT
A NOVEL
ROWENA DAWN
SCARLET LEAF

Mr. (Almost) Right

.

Rowena Dawn

Published by Scarlet Leaf Publishing House, 2020.

This is a work of fiction. Names, characters, places and incidents are products of the author's imagination and are not to be construed as real.

Any resemblance to actual events, locales, organizations or persons, living or dead, is entirely coincidental.

For information address Scarlet Leaf

scarletleafpublishinghouse@gmail.com

Table of Contents

TO SIMONA AND ANDREI

CHAPTER ONE

"UGH," ELLA GROANED and threw a plate toward Colin.

Ella never reached her target, even though she practiced at it often. After all, she had broken enough plates, using Colin as target practice.

However, she hoped she would stop missing and hit him one of those days. The man wasn't such a tiny target, after all.

"Come on, baby! You have to understand," Colin pleaded with his puppy eyes and an imploring gesture; he was a master at doing that.

Ella rolled her eyes, although she felt like skinning him. He would always do that. He would leave her waiting for him like that and take off to be with one of his friends.

She wanted to scream in frustration. In her book, the definition of a boyfriend was eons away from what he offered to her.

Her sister had been right when she said that she had to lose Colin and fast before it was too late. Ella had to find something better soon. Otherwise, she wouldn't have any dishes left in her cupboard.

Last week, she had finished off the beautiful dish set with tiny flowers painted around the rim, and she had loved that set. Ella had bought it during one of her exhausting trips through several antique shops, and she had worked hard to put her little hands on it. Then, she had broken all of them in only one evening like a stupid cow. It was harsh, but that was the truth.

Huh! Well, enough was enough, and Colin could hang. She had better things to do than wait for him and practice her non-existent target skills.

"You know what?" Ella put her fisted hands on her hips and confronted him. "I've just had enough. Go and play with the boys, Colin, and forget you've ever known me, jerk!" By the end of her tirade, Ella had been shouting at the top of her lungs.

Colin cringed when her voice reached the highest note. Yep, she could yell just fine. Her lungs worked well, after all. So, she could scream. So what?

Ella was sick and tired of Colin and his lame excuses. She had accepted Colin's apologies far too often in the past, and now, she regretted her weakness and lack of judgment. She felt like kicking herself, ashamed that she hadn't woken up earlier and seen the truth.

At least, she preferred to think that her behaviour had resulted from temporary blindness and insanity. She would be more intelligent in the future. Otherwise, the only thing left for her was to pull a bag over her head. She wouldn't deserve anything else.

Ella decided that it was high time she had cleared her head. She needed to get out of the sick routine she had been wallowing in lately and grow a backbone. So, that would be the day when she would reclaim her future and love life back.

It wasn't like she would get any younger. She was past her prime. That was what her grandma had said when they met last month. Ella would reach the big forty soon. It was just there, a few years away down the road.

Ella needed to re-think her life. Stuck in that so-called relationship, she had stopped feeling anything. The woman wasn't happy or even somewhat content, so Ella had to let go and look for greener pastures. She couldn't do worse than Colin.

"You can't be serious, baby. Come on! You don't want me to leave. You love me," Colin said and smiled, opening his arms. Once upon a time, his smile made Ella shiver, but not anymore. She felt nothing, and that shocked her.

Suddenly, awareness dawned in—a cold shower for her pride. She had already stopped having any feelings for Colin, if she had ever had any. The man was just one more mistake to count in her life.

Ella didn't feel anything for him, but anger and anger didn't qualify as a feeling. Besides, it wasn't healthy to be angry all the time. After a year of missed dates and lonely evenings spent by herself in her apartment, waiting for Prince Charming to arrive on his white horse, she had nothing left for him.

Yep, Prince Charming was tarnished, Ella mused, watching Colin pensively. Maybe she needed a regular guy to play house with him and build a nuclear family, she thought.

Nah, that wasn't for her either. Ella reconsidered after just a few seconds. She needed sparks and excitement in her life, and she knew now that she wouldn't ever have that with Colin.

Ella still remembered last Christmas. Too embarrassed to call a friend or visit with family, she had spent both Christmas Eve and Christmas Day alone because he couldn't make it. She knew what people would have said and that they had offered tons of advice.

And Colin had gone ice fishing. Or, at least, he had told her so, she frowned, remembering his words. Nevertheless, he wasn't the man to go ice fishing, so she had doubts.

A slave to comfort, Colin wouldn't have spent time at under zero temperature, the wind howling through every crack of a shabby hut. He would pass the time with friends and a few bottles of wine anytime if the conditions were right. Ella could see him in a cozy cabin, fitted with a fireplace and a bar.

However, Colin wouldn't enjoy staying in a rough shed, fishing in a hole dug in the ice. So, that was fishy enough to raise questions, and she hadn't seen it at the time, damn it.

Still, Ella had just gone along with his lies. God knows how many others Colin had fed her along the time. Now Ella knew that she had lost judgment entirely for a time.

Calm, very calm, as nothing had mattered anymore, Ella replied to him, "Yes, I'm serious, Colin. I want you to leave now, and I don't want you to come back ever again."

Colin's eyes measured her with irony, and the corners of his mouth turned up. Ella understood that the man didn't believe that she was serious. Her eyes narrowed to slits, and she looked straight into his eyes. She tilted her head with determination and held her chin high.

"If you do, I'll accuse you of stalking, and you won't like the consequences, Colin. I can assure you," Ella said with confidence. She worked as a paralegal, and she knew the law well.

At his turn, Colin knew that Ella had never changed her mind once she had made a decision. He had even chanced to hear Ella's father saying that the woman was as stubborn as a mule.

Ella might not have agreed with her father openly, but she knew he was right deep down. She was his daughter, after all, and a mule would know a mule when they saw one.

Besides, Ella's voice told Colin that she wasn't joking. That did widen his eyes, and that pushed Ella to give him a firmer nudge so that he would get out of her house. She went to the front door with measured steps and opened it.

"Adios, muchacho," she said in a sarcastic tone of voice.

Colin stared at her with disbelief. He was still riveted to the same spot, unable to move.

Ella's right eyebrow went up, and she pointed toward the corridor to encourage him to move.

"You know you'll regret this, baby. You will, but I'll wait for you to call when you get back to your senses. Because you will," Colin said resignedly.

He went out of the door, his shoulders hunched as if the entire world weighed on him.

"Don't stay glued to the phone, Colin," Ella shouted after him. 'You weasel!' "I won't call you. Once I close this door behind you, I'll forget you have ever existed in this world."

"Your loss," Colin shrugged with indifference, although he still couldn't believe that she risked throwing him out of the door.

The man had always been sure he didn't have to worry about the future of his relationship with Ella. He had thought that he had already bagged it, and Ella's reaction had come as a huge surprise to him.

Colin didn't recognize that new Ella, but he knew the old one very well. Yes, she would throw dishes at him, and she would shout. He admitted that she had the lungs for that. However, he had never felt that he should worry about anything in their relationship or that he had to work on it. Ella was a sure deal. At least, that was what he believed. That new woman he saw disconcerted him, especially because she was ready to cut off her ties to him.

"Maybe," she replied and shrugged with indifference. "But it's definitely yours, baby," she continued, snapping her fingers. After that parting shot, Ella shut the door in his face. She locked it and also latched the chain for good measure.

Ella wasn't afraid that Colin would come back. Still, she needed a final gesture, something symbolic, a final burial of their relationship. Ella was big on signs and symbols, after all.

CHAPTER TWO

ELLA TAPPED HER FOOT nervously. She wasn't entirely satisfied with herself. The young woman disliked how she had handled the breakup with Colin. She had made a mistake showing too much emotion, and that thought bothered her. However, she had already done it, and she couldn't change anything. She shrugged and looked around.

Her eyes fell on the shards scattered all over her living-room carpet. With a sigh, she started picking them up.

'Oh, God, how many times have I done this? Stupid, stupid cow!' It had taken her too much time to learn her lesson.

Ella shook her head in dismay. She couldn't believe that she had been so blind for such a long time. A week is one thing. All right, maybe even a month or two, but not so many months. That wasn't acceptable.

Colin and Ella had been together for over three years now, the two of them. So, three years went down the drain that evening, and only because she had kept her mind in a cloud. She could feel a sort of constriction in her throat, and she feared that she would start crying if she had tried to clear it.

Ella didn't regret that she had shown Colin to the door, but she did regret that she had wasted three years of her life with that selfish jackass.

Colin had just taken her for granted. And why wouldn't he? She was always there, faithfully waiting, whenever he came back to her.

Ella would express her feelings, and quite strongly sometimes. That was true. But then, it wasn't as if he had cared that she would scream like a banshee or throw dishes, aiming at his head.

And the clock was still ticking. And here she was, almost thirty-seven, childless and husbandless.

'*Ugh.*' Ella threw the slivers in the garbage bin and remained standing there, her fists on her hips, looking out the kitchen window. She didn't see anything but just stared into space.

Suddenly, a thought crossed her mind. Ella hesitated for only one second, and then, brimming with anxiety, she ran to the phone and started dialling Joan's number.

Ella and Jo had known each other for ages, even though they weren't very close. Sometimes being different could do that to people.

"Hi, Jo, it's me, Ella. What are you doing tonight?" she asked in a cheery tone of voice.

"Hi," Jo said hesitantly, and then, a long pause ensued.

Ella didn't blame Jo for being circumspect. She might have had a bone to pick up with Jo now and then, but she couldn't be unfair.

Ella hadn't called her friend for ages to ask about her evening. Her call had come like a thunderbolt to poor Jo. She had failed in being a good friend, but she had her reasons.

"I ... don't know," Jo's reply came with some hesitation.

"No plans?" Ella asked, always with enthusiasm in her voice.

Another pause followed, and Ella recalled that Jo was a bit slow when someone surprised her. That was one of the reasons she didn't like to call Jo. She had other reasons, but that one topped the list.

Now Ella needed Jo, though, so she patiently waited for Jo's reply. Jo liked well-thought plans. She didn't like doing anything on the spur of the moment. If someone asked her to make plans for earlier than three days, she would overthink those plans and the person's reasons for eons.

"Why are you asking?" Jo asked after a while.

"Well, I've been thinking, you know. We should go out to a bar or something," Ella chimed in, happy like a magpie.

She had to act like that. Otherwise, she would cry her eyes out, thinking of how stupid she had been, and that wouldn't do. Nothing would make Jo balk faster than someone crying. Ella understood Jo's motives. Both Ella and Jo had problems when it came to comforting someone. Neither one knew what to say or how to react in such circumstances.

'Yep, another pause,' Ella mused.

Jo took her time to dissect the sudden invitation. Ella decided to wait patiently, although she felt a sharp pain in her arm. It wasn't comfortable to hold the phone in the same position for so long.

Ella enjoyed brief and efficient phone conversations. If she wanted to linger over a discussion, she would do it in a place where she could have some coffee or whiskey.

She wasn't one of the fans of that beautiful invention, the phone. Her phone calls didn't go over three minutes, and that only if she had to talk to her mother, who wouldn't accept anything less and would call her on that.

"But what about Colin?" Jo asked with hesitation. She sounded as if she feared asking the wrong question or hearing the answer, and Ella understood Jo's reaction too well.

It wasn't a mystery, after all. Jo wasn't one of Colin's supporters, and she had never made a secret about it. Everyone knew that.

Anyway, Jo wasn't the only one who couldn't stand Colin. The Colin anti-fan club was large enough. If Ella thought better, no one among her family or friends rooted for Colin but her mother.

'The piece of... Okay, not now.'

Ella needed to take care of some more pressing things right then, and she couldn't enjoy trashing Colin. She had to persuade Jo that he wouldn't bother them ever again, and they could have fun together.

If she failed, her plans would follow the route of her broken relationship. They would also go right down the drain.

"You shouldn't worry about that, Jo. Colin's got his ticket," she assured her friend, always in that joyful tone of voice that sounded slightly artificial in her ears and left her with a sour taste in her mouth. Nevertheless, she crossed her fingers, hoping that Jo would buy it.

"What kind of ticket?" Jo asked with bafflement, and Ella could imagine her wide, shocked eyes. Her friend's voice revealed Jo's bewilderment.

"I meant that I broke up with him for good, Jo. Now, I want to go on a hunt, and you're my wingman or girl or whatever!" Ella shouted cheerily. For a moment there, she could imagine Jo cringed. Of course, another pause followed in their conversation.

'Come on, Jo, live up a little, girl! Maybe we can go out before we're fifty. At least, that was my plan,' Ella thought.

"What do you want to hunt?" another hesitant answer came, and Ella felt like grinding her teeth.

Jo needed to go out more and mingle with people more often. She didn't have any imagination and never understood a metaphor.

"A man, Jo. What the heck else? I want to hunt a man. A regular man to have children with," Ella shouted, forgetting that she needed to be tactful to make Jo cooperate with her plans and go out with her.

She had talked too fast, so Ella had to stop and breathe. That helped her reconsider her prickly attitude, and she promised herself to show more patience. After all, Jo wasn't to blame that Ella's plans for the future had crumbled.

Now Jo decided to chime in. "Now? You want to make children now?"

"No, you... you, Jo!" Ella spluttered, unable to find her words. She forgot everything about tact and patience.

"Not now, like in right now. It's not like I'm going to a guy and say: 'Make me a child or more if possible!'" she practically shouted, losing the last threads of patience she had.

Jo could drive her mad with just a few words. That never changed.

"But I want to find a man with whom I could have children. Let's say sometime next year," she continued in a more reasonable tone of voice.

"Oh, I see. I see. And what can I do?" Jo asked her.

"I don't know!" Ella shouted and thought, stupid, stupid, stupid. "I suppose you could come with me to a singles bar. That would be a start in my hunt."

Pause at the other end of the line, of course, what else. That pain in Ella's arm became sharper, and Ella mentally sent an arrow in Jo's direction. She visualized it, piercing Jo straight through her heart. No, better through her brain. Jo's heart was in the right place most of the time. Her friend's brain caused the damn problem.

"All right, Ella. When?" Jo finally accepted her friend's invitation.

'Next century, you dummy!' Ella thought unkindly. Nevertheless, she replied sweetly. "Tonight. I'll come and get you at eight, okay?"

"I suppose," Jo hesitated.

'Damn, she's slow!' Ella thought. However, she knew that Jo's hesitance wasn't about being slow but unsure.

"Okay, eight it is. See you, girl. Bye!" Ella spoke fast so that Jo wouldn't have the time to reconsider anything.

Exhausted, Ella hurried to disconnect the call. Throwing plates was not an easy job. Throwing your boyfriend – all right, ex-boyfriend, out of the house, wasn't easy either. Talking to Jo – well, that would try even a saint.

CHAPTER THREE

ELLA DIDN'T DARE TAKE any chances, so she arrived at Jo's apartment five minutes earlier. She remembered that punctuality was one of Jo's best qualities if one would think of that as a good quality in certain circumstances. Jo was a stickler for promptness. God forbid someone would be one minute late! The quiet Jo would switch to nagging Jo, and the culprit's ears would catch fire.

Ella had had her runs in with Jo on that subject before, and tonight, she only wanted to have fun. Being lectured as if she were a ten-year-old, who had forgotten the rules, didn't come into her plans.

She kept her eyes on her watch and knocked on Jo's door only two minutes before eight. After long consideration, Ella concluded that she had better give Jo time for the final touches on her ensemble or whatever she would wear that evening.

No one caught Jo without perfect makeup, clothes, and accessories. She would get upset if Ella knocked at her door before she had every hair under control.

Nevertheless, Ella couldn't wait to see what Jo put together. Her friend was high on the fashion scale and always a delight to watch.

Ella didn't mind Jo's obsession with clothes, hairstyle, and so on. She even thought it was good for her if Jo liked to look perfect.

However, it wasn't so good that she asked the same thing to everyone else. Ella didn't have enough patience with such things.

If she remembered correctly, that had been the reason for their last squabble. Ella was supposed to meet Jo at a restaurant and was running late, so she didn't have time to change home from work. She showed up in a yellow sundress at the restaurant Jo had chosen, and her friend disliked Ella's toilet on the spot.

Jo turned her nose up at Ella's dress, pointing out that Ella didn't dress for the venue. Jo considered that Ella's slovenliness threw a shadow over her, as well. Hence, she lectured Ella at length about consideration and respect.

That was when Ella left the restaurant. She didn't throw any plates at that time because she wasn't at home, after all. Still, she threw some choice words over her shoulder, and not words she would usually say.

Jo frowned upon the way Ella chose to express her anger. Later, Ella had to admit that Jo's reaction had been expected.

Ella had let herself a little carried away that day, and even now, she grimaced when she remembered about it. Her mother would have washed her mouth with soap if she had known what had come out of Ella's mouth.

More important, even though her friend was a pain in the ass sometimes, Jo didn't deserve to be talked like that. For days afterward, Ella had felt guilty for treating her friend that way.

However, they made up a few months later. Of course, Ella apologized for her rudeness, although it took her a while to admit that she could have handled things better. It took her a little more to gather her courage and call Jo to apologize.

Still, Jo's priggishness was burnt in Ella's brain. She knew a faux pas might make Jo go right back inside her apartment and leave Ella at the door.

Ella was planning to enjoy that night. She didn't have a clear plan, just a foggy idea about how she would have liked things to evolve. She was thinking of having the night of her life, or something on those lines, at least.

However, Ella knew that it was important not to upset Jo in any way if she wanted to be successful in her quest. An upset Jo meant that the night would turn into a total loss, even if Ella would persuade her friend to come with her to the bar.

Not even the bravest of men would have dared to approach the two of them if sparks were in full swing, and that would have defeated Ella's purpose to go out and on the hunt.

As a respectable Swiss clock, Jo was ready to go when Ella finally considered that it was the right time to knock on her door. Ella had expected nothing less from her.

Jo opened the door, wearing a beautiful black cocktail dress. It was a knock-out dress meant to turn heads or make weaker men walk into walls. Jo looked just gorgeous, and they wouldn't be able to take their eyes from her. That wouldn't have been something new or out of the ordinary. Ella had seen it happen in the past, and more than once.

She couldn't deny that Jo looked terrific. However, Ella repressed the urge to roll her eyes when she glanced at Jo's outfit. It was a little over the top for their destination. Even so, Ella still felt some tinges of envy, which she stifled immediately.

'We're going to a singles bar, Jo, not to a fancy reception,' she mutely reprimanded her friend in her mind.

But Jo was Jo, and no one could have told her anything like that. Ella didn't have a death wish, so she didn't think of speaking her thoughts out loud.

She knew how her friend viewed her. Jo believed that Ella belonged at the bottom of the fashion chain. None of her opinions about that subject mattered. Anyway, Ella never felt the urge to comment on Jo's attire. Jo wasn't someone with whom she would trifle.

Ella now felt a strong desire to find a decent guy and eventually get in the family way. Starting a war about style with Jo was very far from her thoughts.

Her thoughts shocked Ella for a second when they registered in her mind. 'Getting in the family way' sounded very old-fashioned in her ears. Her ideas were a little troubling.

Ella stopped and argued with herself. She had never really thought that she was growing old, but if her thoughts had already taken that path, she had to reconsider that. She shook herself off mentally to get back to reality and shooed the thoughts away.

It wasn't fun to reflect on that perspective too much, even though she knew that natural laws worked against her.

Jo and Ella made a striking duo. Jo was tall and slim with a rich mane of blond hair, which didn't come from a bottle. She had been born with it, as she had been born with long shapely legs. Her short cocktail dress displayed them beautifully—miles and miles of legs that would make people either admire or hate her.

Jo's looks would draw a lot of envy her way, but then she didn't care about what people thought about her. She was self-confident enough, and she never paid attention to anyone. Her opinion was the only one that counted.

Ella liked to think that she knew her friend quite well. Nevertheless, she had never been sure if Jo realized that not everybody admired and loved her.

Short, curvy, and dark-haired, Ella was the total opposite of Jo. She kept her hair short because she didn't have the patience to fuss with it.

Ella had understood from her friends that that required a lot of dedication. Time to tend to a thick, long mane wasn't in Ella's daily planner.

However, she was proud of her hair. It had a healthy shine, and it was thick enough to draw people's eyes her way.

Ella did contemplate letting her hair grow now and then, but her practical side took care to squash the thought on the spot.

So, she kept her hair short, the same pixie style she had adopted in high school, which had served her for years. She could wash it quickly, and she was good to go. She didn't have to waste time to dry it. She just rubbed it with a towel, passed a comb through it, and that was the sum of her efforts.

Ella's dress fell to her knees. She knew she couldn't compete in the leg department with Jo, and she had never tried. After all, she was a rational woman, and she didn't indulge in such thoughts.

Ella had inherited her grandmother's shape. She had everything in abundance, and she was painfully aware of that every so often. Sometimes, and especially when she had the blues, she thought that everything on her was in too much abundance.

Although not round in the wrong places, the mirror showed an excessively stacked and round shape. That was some bliss in disguise, at least.

During her school years, Ella had hated her figure. Her breasts got bigger, her hips rounder, and her derriere was just a little too generous for her taste. She dieted and tried all types of exercising, but nothing seemed to work.

Once she accepted her curvy shape and decided that she looked good, she started enjoying her life and never looked back again.

She could count her college years as the best of her life. They proved that people should be more than mere Xerox copies. Variety had its purpose, after all.

Ella appreciated the contrast with Jo and didn't envy her silhouette, even though Jo gave the impression that she had come out of the pages of a fashion magazine. Whenever the two of them would enter a bar or a club, all eyes turned to them and glimmered with speculation. She knew that they would attract a lot of attention. That was why Ella had decided to invite Jo to go with her.

If she went by herself, she might have got lost amongst the fish in the barrel or attracted only one or two guys, probably the weird ones, as her luck had turned to be lately. She thought of Colin, and her heart cringed. That man proved her luck in that department.

"Look at you," Jo said, perusing Ella's attire and shaking her head. "I think you look all right. That dress isn't what I'd have chosen for you, but ...."

Ella forced a smile on her lips, although she felt the impulse to smack the perfectly painted face of her friend. She had just known that Jo would say something like that. She had tried to steel herself against the indirect insult, but it hurt all the same.

Anyway, that night, Ella was determined to score. Still, she thought that she needed Jo's presence for that, even though sometimes it was difficult to get over her friend's veiled insults. So, she smiled some more and didn't retaliate.

Ironically, Jo wasn't even aware that she offended people with her comments. That had surprised Ella a lot and made her see her friend in a different light. However, Ella didn't understand how it was possible that someone as smart as Jo could be so blind and didn't understand the result of her actions.

"You look awesome," Ella replied to Jo, and she didn't lie. She did believe that Jo looked fabulous, even though she seemed a bit too elegant for a singles bar.

That dress did shout, *'Look at this beautiful piece of art,'* and Jo was indeed a contemporary Venus. Everyone shared that opinion, even Jo's enemies.

Looking at Jo's dress, Ella thought she didn't mind it. She wouldn't be the one who paraded through a bar in a dress more appropriate for a cocktail party.

The two women hugged distantly and kissed the air near each other's cheek – that was the fashion for Jo. However, Ella didn't mind her friend's attitude. She wasn't very out-going either. Ella considered that hugs were meant either for one's lover or family members if she hadn't seen them for a long while.

Ella's family had never been very demonstrative, and she could count her mother's hugs on the fingers of one hand. Her father might have hugged her when she had moved out of the house and rented a flat in Toronto, but she wasn't very sure if that was a fact or a fabricated memory.

An accurate memory was seeing her father come back home from work, plop on the sofa to watch a game, and shut everyone else out. That image had remained engraved on her retina.

Everything else was borderline recollection. It might have happened or not.

Probably Ella felt comfortable with Jo most of the time because of how she had been raised.

Jo didn't ask for hugs and never asked to be comforted. That was another of Ella's shortcomings. She didn't know how to soothe someone, so Jo was the perfect friend. She didn't need soothing or reassurance, and hugging was as alien to her as it was to Ella.

They took the elevator downstairs to the parking lot, and all the while, Jo talked about her work, her family, and friends. She did like to fill in the silence, and seldom someone had the chance to get a word in.

However, Jo didn't expect any answers or opinions. Jo had unyielding views, and she didn't need either approval or advice. So, if Ella didn't feel like listening, she could merely nod now and then, and everything would be fine. Jo was none the wiser that she was talking all by herself.

"So, where are we going?" Jo asked once she was comfortably seated in Ella's car, and she had carefully fastened her seatbelt.

"Well, I heard that a new bar opened on Willow Street a few days ago. The ambiance is nice, although a bit eclectic," Ella replied offhand, and then she turned the engine on. "So, I thought we'd go there," she said but avoided looking at Jo.

"Define eclectic?" Jo asked, looking at Ella through her narrowed eyes.

Ella didn't expect less. Jo would always do that when she had the feeling that something was fishy or someone was trying to play a trick on her.

Showing the first signs of anxiety that evening, Ella fidgeted in her seat for a few moments. The singles bar she had in mind wasn't one of Jo's usual arenas, and Ella knew that. Anyway, Ella didn't intend to go to one of the bars Jo enjoyed. The young woman could have stayed at home just fine because she would have just wasted that evening anyway.

Ella was looking for a real man, not one of those tie-wearing guys who talked a big game and delivered zilch. She had had her share of such guys in the past. She wanted a chance to put her life back on track, so she needed to change the game's variables.

Now, she didn't have anything against a guy in a suit and a tie. That was fine with her, but it also depended on the guy.

It would have been great to find a financially stable man with a good job, and so on. That didn't mean that she had to choose someone based only on those criteria, though.

Of course, she excluded bums, interested in finding a woman to keep them from the start. She refused to pay for a man's living expenses, and she wasn't so old that she would settle just for anyone. It was a principle she didn't intend to forget any time soon, if ever.

Anyway, she had thought that it would be good to mix things, and the bar she had chosen offered a lot of choices. She had heard that executives and lawyers, some fighters, and blue-collar guys came there.

The problem with Jo was that she would look down on the fighters and the blue-collar guys.

They were going to a singles bar so that Ella could meet Mr. Right or, more realistically, Mr. Almost Right. Nevertheless, Ella didn't choose to go to that bar with Jo's preferences in mind. What Jo wanted was just peripheral. That was Ella's night.

"Well, I think it means that you can find all sorts of people, like executives, and accountants, and dentists, and... I don't know, let's say, artists...."

Now Ella was stretching the truth big time, and she knew she would be paying for that later.

Jo didn't like to rub her elbows with the blue-collar class. That was universal knowledge and probably written somewhere in Jo's Bible.

The young woman was always looking for an executive or medical practitioner. Such a man could offer her the world in an oyster.

That didn't mean that Jo was a materialist. She made enough to live on, so she didn't look for a man to provide her with dough or other things. Yet, she was an elitist.

Ella was more down-to-earth. She didn't care about a guy's profession, but she cared a lot about a guy's character, habits, and reliability.

After her long hiatus with Colin, a well-known podiatrist, she was keen to find a reliable man. She didn't give a fig about his social status.

If the guy was a plumber or a lawyer, it was the same thing for her, although she might have inclined toward the plumber.

A lawyer would be away most of the time, and she had already been alone long enough. She wanted something else.

Besides, most lawyers she had met in her profession didn't like to tell the truth too much. They were very good at playing with it, which was a deal-breaker for her. She was sick of the lies Colin had fed her during the last few years.

Jo kept her eyes on Ella as if she knew that she was fiddling with the truth. Ella fought hard to keep her composure under Jo's stare. It was enough time for Jo to see what eclectic meant once they got to the bar.

Anyway, Jo still could hook with a wealthy executive there. Some men like that came down there for the music and good drinks. So Jo had a chance to find the man of her dreams. Once Jo had told Ella that she would wait out for the perfect man. Ella had her doubts that a perfect man existed somewhere in the world.

Ella pretended to hone in on the traffic, so she didn't have to pay too much attention to Jo and answer uncomfortable questions.

"What if you drink?" Jo resumed her questions.

"What do you mean?" Ella glanced confused to Jo for a second and then returned her eyes to the road stretching before them.

"You're driving, and if you drink, we won't be able to get back home," her friend pointed out in her lecture mode.

"No worries, mommy," Ella countered. "We can call a taxi anytime, and I can come back for my car tomorrow," Ella explained.

She barely concealed her grimace. She tightened her teeth, squashing a couple of curses under her tongue.

"Or who knows, we might land some awesome guys, and the transportation problem," she stressed out the word with irony, "would be moot," Ella thought to say.

Jo seemed to consider her answer, and then, she turned her steely eyes to Ella.

"If you drink, even if you drink only one glass, we take a taxi," Jo said in a tone that forbade any further negotiations.

Ella sighed with disappointment. By then, Jo should have known that Ella never drove when she drank. They had been friends most of their lives, and Jo's lack of knowledge about her character was somewhat unsettling.

Once more, Jo proved that she didn't bother to remember anything about Ella's life or personality. Ella wondered what the heck Jo knew about her or if she bothered to know anything else besides her name, phone number, and how she looked.

Ella also berated herself for not taking a taxi from the start. She should have known better.

She knew she would drink nothing else but non-alcoholic beer. She needed her mental faculties unimpaired to succeed in her project. However, for Jo, even that non-alcoholic beer meant that Ella drank, and the result would be the same. They still had to take a taxi back home, and Ella could have spared herself some trouble.

"We'll take a taxi, Jo, don't worry. I'll pay for night parking, and that's it," she conceded just to be rid of that subject.

She hoped that the rest of the trip would be silent, and she wouldn't have to fence any more unpleasant questions.

It just wasn't her day, though. Jo filled with irrelevant chatter the entire thirty-five-minute drive to the club. Luckily, Ella could turn a deaf ear to the prattle and pretend it was background noise.

CHAPTER FOUR

JO THOUGHT THAT MAKING an entrance when going somewhere was better, and she did know to create one. The two young women stopped just beyond the threshold after they entered the bar so that the people inside would notice them and have a good look at them.

Nevertheless, although the two women looked stunning together, only a few guys looked their way. All the others were involved in other things and didn't bother to shift their eyes at them.

Ella's hopes plummeted hard. It was hard not to notice the lack of interest, and she barely kept her smile on her lips to save face.

However, among those who glanced, one appeared interested enough to wink at them. Now, Ella didn't know at which one of them he winked, but she smiled brightly at him all the same.

The man didn't look bad at all. However, his dishevelled blond hair and rugged jeans, which hugged his hips just a tad too tight, labelled him a bad boy.

In Ella's book, bad boys were good when you were young and wild and wanted to experiment and live life like tomorrow would never come. Such guys weren't so good for a woman trying to bring her life back on track, start a family, and have children.

But, what the heck, he was good to look at, and at least, Ella could look. She still admired a broad chest and sculpted abs, even if she got older.

The white t-shirt hugged the man's hard body like a second skin. Ella didn't doubt that the man liked working out regularly.

That was somewhat discouraging for Ella. She rarely had a chance with such guys. They just glanced at her and concluded that she didn't have a healthy life. Immediately, they would look away, uninterested.

That was a pity, though. In fact, Ella worked hard for a healthy life, although she didn't go to a gym regularly.

She hated to mix with the fairies, as she called the skinny girls, who usually filled the gyms and judged her because of her full figure. Ella was comfortable with who she was and how she looked, but she preferred to avoid unpleasantness if possible.

Nevertheless, she exercised every day for health reasons, running up and down the stairs. Ella spent a considerable chunk of her day in a chair. So, she had decided to balance her sedentary office life by taking the stairs instead of an elevator right from the beginning of her professional life.

Ella also took long walks every day and even swam as much as possible. She did that regularly, at least three times a week, although sometimes it was challenging to fit a swim in her busy schedule every day. Besides that, she trained in a dojo, with some regularity.

She knew she looked good enough. Yet, those fit guys overlooked her, and she didn't understand why. Ella shrugged and started toward a table.

Jo followed her, looking around with skepticism. She measured the few guys dressed in suits, and her brows knitted. None of those men seemed appropriate. Once seated, Jo turned her eyes to the enormous room once more and then turned to Ella.

"I don't think that you've made the right choice for tonight, Ella. I don't see many eligible guys in here."

"Probably, there aren't any," Ella answered with indifference. "But keep an open mind, Jo," she pleaded. "And please, don't forget, I haven't chosen this bar for a good selection for you, but for me. I told you that I have a definite plan," she said, also sitting down.

Then, trying to relax, she took the menu off the table to see what she could order.

"Well, I can understand that, of course, but I don't think you'd find the right man here, Ella. You need to look for someone with some class, someone different from Colin," Jo insisted, not ready to let the subject drop already.

"Different from Colin is the motto of the day, Jo. Believe me," Ella answered emphatically.

At the same time, she busied herself with making her selections from her menu.

"However, that means that I'm looking for someone eligible in my eyes, not yours. I can't stress that enough. You know we have different tastes, Jo," Ella replied.

She took her eyes off the menu and looked straight into Jo's eyes. Her friend wasn't there to choose for Ella. She needed to make sure that Jo understood her place that evening. Her role consisted in offering some company.

Jo scowled at her but refrained from saying anything and took the other menu off the table, as well. She perused the entrees first and then the drinks, turning her nose to some of them.

"I don't even know half of these," she exclaimed. "What are you going to order?" she asked Ella. Jo was puzzled and couldn't make up her mind.

"Well, you know me. When in doubt, go with what you know. So, I'll order a cheeseburger with fries and a non-alcoholic beer for the beginning. Then, I'll move to the triple chocolate cake and a soft drink."

"My, can you eat all that?" Jo wondered.

Ella glanced at her with narrowed eyes and said, "Yes, I can, Jo, and so could you if you were in my shoes. I haven't eaten anything all day. However, I don't compete for the skinniest girl in the land, Jo. I leave that to you if you want. You know very well that I don't like to pretend that I'm something I am not."

"I know, but ... wouldn't that chase the guys away? And you said you're in a hurry ... the children and so on ...."

"I am, but that doesn't mean that I'd pretend to be someone I'm not. What good would that do to me in the long run? I wouldn't be able to eat just salad or fruit pieces all my life, would I?" Ella snapped at Jo.

A second later, her eyes fell on the man she had noticed at their arrival in the bar. He was there near their table, listening to them, a massive grin on his face. He had been there for a while and enjoyed himself. However, they had been so deep in their argument that they hadn't seen him.

Ella felt like hiding under the table, but not before hitting Jo over the head, possibly with a boulder. Jo constantly nagged her over unimportant things, making her forget about the important ones, like noticing a hunk standing near their table.

The man stretched his hand to her. With cheer in his voice, he said, "I'm Mark."

She glanced at his hand first and then back to his eyes. She half expected to see a mocking smile in his gaze, and she was pleasantly surprised to notice that he didn't try to mock her.

She shook his hand, saying, "I'm Ella. And this here," she tilted her head toward her friend, "is my friend, Jo."

The man tried to shake Jo's hand as well, but Jo just turned her nose in the air and pretended not to notice his gesture. That made Ella furious. She had never excused such snobbish behaviour.

"Jo," she practically growled to her friend, and her outburst made Mark grin again.

For a moment there, Mark worried that he had made a mistake going to their table. He hadn't expected the women to discount him as fast as yesterday's newspaper. Yet, the man was lucky. He had been interested in Ella from the beginning, and she wasn't distant like her girlfriend. Her attitude toward him and her smile made him feel at ease.

"All right, all right," Jo protested to what she qualified as Ella's lack of decorum. "I'm Jo," she said with animosity and shook Mark's hand. However, she didn't bother to hide her displeasure.

"So, would you, girls, mind if I joined you?" he asked, always smiling at Ella and trying not to look at her friend.

"Yes," Jo said.

"No," said Ella at the same time, and her friendly smile turned into a frown when she realized what her friend had said.

"What the heck, Jo?" she inquired in a crisp tone, looking at her friend with steely eyes. Ella thought she had been very clear from the beginning. She had already explained to Jo that she had a specific goal in mind, and the choices would be hers, not Jo's.

Jo shrugged with indifference and said, "Fine with me. If you want him to stay, of course, he can stay, but if you ask me …."

"I'm not asking you," Ella interrupted her with a scowl.

Then she turned to Mark and asked sweetly, "Would you like to have a seat at our table, Mark?"

She might have sounded sweet, but the metallic glint in her eyes told him that she was angry, and he didn't want to be the recipient of her fury. Other than that, the women's argument amused him, so he nodded, taking a seat next to Ella.

He had noticed their arrival in the bar. He had made an effort not to whistle at the striking pair. They were as different as night and day, and the small one, the black-haired pixie one, was an absolute delight for his eyes.

The woman seemed to be what he wanted in a woman. That was evident when she stood next to her friend.

"So, what would you like to order?" he asked Ella, focusing on her as if Jo hadn't even been there.

Jo narrowed her eyes when understanding dawned on her. It was her turn to be shunned, and she didn't expect or accept that.

Jo was confident that people wanted to be with her. Her company was always coveted and considered much better than Ella's.

'What could you expect from a guy in jeans?' she thought and smirked. However, her behaviour didn't pass unnoticed by the other two.

"Anything wrong, Jo?" Ella asked sweetly again, maybe a little too sweetly for comfort.

Mark guessed that the woman would react like a mean cat if pushed enough, and although he didn't understand his reasons, he enjoyed that thought.

Ella knew very well what Jo was thinking. It wasn't the first time she slighted someone just because they didn't wear the CO powerful suit. As if those CO guys would live their entire life dressed that way, with a tie around their neck. That was just a wrong, narrow view of the world. Ella knew that those guys had to decompress now and then. To do that, they had to lose the suit.

"No, everything's fine. But if you think you can manage by yourself, I'd go and meet some friends. I told them I'd try to pass by if I had the time," Jo replied with a princely air, which said, *'nothing you're doing can touch me.'*

Ella had already had enough of Jo's airs for one evening and decided to cut her friend's exit short. So, she answered with nonchalance. "Then don't let us keep you, Jo. If you have other engagements, you definitely must honour them. We'll do just fine, the two of us, won't we, Mark?" she turned to Mark with a smile on her lips.

Mark noticed that the smile didn't reach the woman's eyes. The young woman was tense like a string. He grinned and nodded his approval to make her feel more at ease.

The new evolution of events was more than fine with him anyway. He could feel that Jo disliked him, although he didn't know the reason behind her behaviour. He didn't have difficulties with women, as a rule. All right, he did, but not that kind of problem.

Women were eager to climb all over him, and he didn't know if it was because they wanted him, the man, or his status and money. He had had his history with both types of women, and after a while, he stopped caring. He took what he wanted from them and didn't give a damn in return.

Jo said her goodbyes, but not before sending a reproachful look toward Ella. She was sure that the guy didn't deserve her friend's waste of time, and she pitied Ella for falling so easy in his arms.

She understood that Ella had started to feel that her biological clock was ticking. Nonetheless, that didn't mean to forget decorum and breed, in Jo's opinion. Differences would surface when one didn't expect them, and consequences would be unpleasant and disruptive. That wouldn't lead to a happily ever after.

CHAPTER FIVE

GUILT SNEAKED IN ELLA'S heart for sending Jo away. However, Jo's presence would have ruined the evening. She disliked Mark, and she didn't want that Ella talked to him.

Ella watched Jo leave the bar, and then she turned to Mark. To her surprise, the man had kept his eyes on her, not on her friend. Mark's disinterest in Jo's long legs astounded her. The man watched Ella intently, and that made her nervous.

"Is anything wrong with me? Maybe I have something on my face," she brushed her fingers over her cheeks. "You're staring. You know that, don't you?" she said.

Mark shook his head. "Are you ready to order?" he asked her. "I was ready to order when you arrived. But there you were, so I forgot about food. That doesn't mean that I'm not still hungry," he added with a grin and winked at her.

"You've already heard what I want, haven't you?" she asked him. She tilted her head, gazing at him through narrowed eyes. She thought he would deny it, and she would catch him lying.

"Yep, I have," he nodded. "Cheeseburger, fries, a triple chocolate cake, and non-alcoholic beer," Mark rattled off Ella's order. "Did I get it right?"

She agreed, and he chuckled, waving to the waitress to come and take their order. Ella didn't know what to make of him, so she decided to wait and see.

The waitress sashayed to their table, a broad smile for Mark on her lips. She ignored Ella, and the young woman's good mood evaporated. She measured the server with sharp eyes.

The waitress was the kind of woman who made men's hearts race faster. Such women always threw a shadow over Ella's head, and that was the last thing she wanted right then.

"We'll take two cheeseburgers with fries, two non-alcoholic beers, and two triple chocolate cakes," Mark said in a matter-of-fact tone of voice. Then he turned back to Ella, dismissing the server, and Ella felt better.

She didn't know if he had done it for her benefit. However, she liked Mark's attitude.

Colin would have flirted with the waitress as if Ella hadn't even been there. That always angered her.

The waitress left with a pout, and a rude comment popped into Ella's mind. She wasn't mean, but she didn't understand why waitresses always ignored her and paid attention only to her male companion. Their attitude said, 'You don't count. Get lost.'

"So, let's get to know each other better," Mark proposed, and her eyes widened.

Surprised, Ella didn't know what to say. She had been out of the dating scene for almost three years now. Besides, the woman hadn't dated much before.

Growing mainly among boys, she hadn't learned any flirting skills, and that had been a handicap for her. She had probably settled for Colin because of that.

At the expression on her face, Mark burst into laughter and patted her hand.

"Don't get spooked out, Ella. That wasn't a come-on, I swear," he shook his head, his lips curving upward. That mischievous grin added a new dimension to his bad-boy image. "I'm just saying that we could share some things. You know. We should have a first-date conversation. We can talk about what we do for a living, or about your favourite colour; if you like to read and what. Things like that," he waved his hand negligently.

His playful tone eased the woman's tension away, and she breathed deeply.

"All right then," she answered. "I can do that. Let's see. I'm a paralegal. I love green, and I read thrillers and romance, peppered with erotica. Does that answer your question?" she asked, and she lifted her brows.

"Yep, you've exhausted three of my questions in under a minute. I wonder what else we could do tonight," Mark replied with a chuckle.

"You could give me your answers," she winked at him, his demeanour encouraging her to be bold. Ella was daring enough in other matters, but she felt awkward with men. She rarely knew the right thing to say or do.

"Yes, I could do that," he nodded. "You're right. So, here it goes," he breathed deeply. "I'm in business. I also like green. So, we match in colours. And I read thrillers. Hey, not bad at all. We do have some interests in common, after all," he said in an amused tone of voice.

Even though he didn't want a serious relationship, Mark considered that a couple should share some interests. At least, they could argue about the characters of a book during a rainy evening when they felt lazy and didn't want to get off the couch and go out.

"So, before getting into serious stuff, like talking about books, are you a regular here?" he asked her.

Ella opened her mouth to answer but saw the waitress arrive with their order. The fast service surprised her.

"Look, our order is here. I'm famished, so sorry, but I'll have to tackle that burger first. We'll get into that serious stuff later."

"Good for you," Mark said. "I do like a girl with a good appetite. I dated a vegetarian once," he said in a pensive tone of voice. "Our choices in food were a source of arguments. I tried to give up meat, and I managed to stick to that decision for about two weeks. But come on, I need my meat load to function," he shrugged. "You know how it is. Our relationship died of natural causes," he said.

He made room for the waitress to unload her tray on the table. The waitress smiled sweetly at him while taking care of his food and arranging it in front of him just so. When she served Ella, the smile vanished promptly, as if someone took a sponge and erased it from her lips.

The server looked at the heap of fries on Ella's plate, and then, her eyes shifted pointedly at the woman's hips. She shook her head with a fake regret.

"Yes, I eat fries, and I have no remorse," Ella said.

Her words shocked the waitress. She hadn't expected a direct attack.

Mark had already noticed the waitress's silently ragging on Ella and was getting ready to say something. Ella's reply made him chuckle.

The server straightened her shoulders and asked, "Will that be all? Would you like anything else?"

Both shook their heads and murmured a perfunctory 'Thank you.' The woman left in a huff, swinging her narrow hips nervously.

"I won't order anything else even if I starve," Ella whispered to Mark. "I've heard it's not a good idea to upset your waitress. Thank God she brought the cakes too."

"Yeah, I know," Mark whispered at his turn. "However, she was rude, so she deserved it. Still, I'm thankful that you've waited to see the food on the table. If not, we'd have had to go and look for another place to eat, and I've already had my heart set on this burger. I saw it on someone's plate earlier," he confessed with a twinkle in his eyes.

They laughed, and Ella punched Mark as if they had been friends for ages. She was carefree with him, and that surprised her. She hadn't experienced that feeling in a long time.

Colin had made Ella tense and angry for the last few months. She had forgotten to have fun. Terrible stomachaches and migraines pestered her, and she would be out of sorts for days. Only anger fuelled some of her days.

"You're a mean one," Mark observed, turning her attention back to him again. "And I like it. You're not afraid of saying what you think, and that's a good thing."

She shrugged and bit into her juicy cheeseburger. Focused on the taste exploding on her tongue, she didn't notice that she made a sound. The burger was tasty, she was hungry, and she moaned with pleasure.

However, Mark's eyes got fixed on her mouth. Ella's full lips, as well as the tip of her tongue, snaking out and licking them now and then, fascinated him. He kept staring at her while she took small bites and chewed silently. It was as if she put a spell on him, and his cheeseburger lay forgotten on his plate.

Ella finally observed that he was gawking at her and felt awkward. Her brows bunched together, and she swallowed fast.

"Don't tell me you're one of those guys who get turned on by watching a full-figure woman eat," she said in a grim tone of voice.

That was her worst nightmare. She had heard about people like that. They found pleasure either in watching fat people eat or feeding them.

Ella had always managed to avoid such groups. She wasn't fat, but she wasn't skinny either. The young woman packed a few more pounds than she should have. However, she didn't need or want to get involved in that world.

Ella needed a healthy relationship that involved talking and laughter. She wasn't in her seventies yet, so she also wanted good sex. She wished to walk down the aisle and tie the knot in the end.

She hadn't thought about what came after the wedding. She couldn't imagine her married life without having Mr. Right, or Mr. Almost Right, before her eyes. Nevertheless, she wanted to have children and share a comfortable life with a man she loved.

Ella continued to stare at Mark with a frown. He finally got over his shock and shook his head in disbelief.

"No, don't worry about that," he waved his hand. "I'm not into that culture. I do like curves. That's true. Otherwise, I wouldn't have made a pass on you. Anyways, I was watching you because you moaned. Moans have a strange effect on my pants. They get a tad tighter," Mark replied.

Ella blushed and bit her lower lip, looking at him from under her lashes. She didn't have any experience with blunt talking. Colin had never talked to her like that, and besides him, she had had only two boyfriends. Neither of the two had said something like that either. Ella wondered if Mark wasn't out of her league.

Nevertheless, she had to reconsider the appeal of such talking. She liked it. Something feverish ran through her veins, and she felt alive. That hadn't happened for a while. Lately, she had gone through life on auto-pilot. She had missed that special thing that made life unique and sparkling like a bottle of good champagne.

She hadn't felt antsy and full of expectations for some time now. Not that Colin had given her too much magic, except for the first two months.

Still, that was also her fault. Tired of looking around, she had settled for Colin. That had been a mistake. Nonetheless, she had fought to make that relationship work with dogged determination. Her free-running mouth had always made holding onto a relationship impossible.

"I see the cat got your tongue," Mark teased her with a satisfied grin on his lips, taking his burger off his plate. A mischievous light shone in his eyes. He took a large bite and started chewing.

Ella didn't know what to say or do, so she picked up her beer and washed her throat. She shut her eyes, trying to regroup. After a few seconds, she opened her eyes and flinched. Mark nearly touched her. He had braced his elbows on the table, leaning over her.

"How do you feel about dancing?" he asked her in a whisper.

Ella practically winced. She had expected something else. She stared at him, and then, her eyes turned to the designated dance rink. There, several couples moved in the rhythm of a steamy blues.

Two couples stood out for entirely different reasons, and Ella's brows hiked up her forehead. They were swaying in the rhythm of the music. However, one of the couples was making out in the middle of the floor, seriously engrossed in each other. The other couple was just as entranced in their passion. Their hands wandered all over each other.

Ella glanced back at Mark and caught him staring at her again, and this time, she wasn't eating. Her burger had been long forgotten on her plate.

"Now what?" she asked.

"Nothing," he shrugged. "I just think you'd like to dance," he lifted his left shoulder. "I'm just waiting for you to say it."

"Really? And what makes you think...."

"You're tapping your foot in the rhythm of the music. You're drumming your fingers on the table," he interrupted her, waving his hand.

"Ah, that. I haven't noticed," Ella replied with nonchalance. However, she chided herself for her lack of control.

"But you'd like to dance, wouldn't you?" Mark replied, keeping his eyes trained on her.

"You want to dance with me," she murmured, staring at him. His insistence on the topic puzzled her. Guys rarely wanted to dance.

"Yes, I want to dance with you. Now. Right here," Mark specified. "So, what are you saying?"

"Don't you want to eat your food first? Before it gets cold?" she pointed to his plate.

He looked at her for a few seconds and then glanced back at his plate. He appeared to consider her question, and she hoped he would want to finish eating first.

It was never a smart thing to leave your food or drinks unattended on the table in a place where you had never been before, and you didn't know anybody.

"All right, Ella, let's eat so we can dance. I've got a hankering to dance with you tonight," he winked at her.

She felt antsy again. The man's attitude was disconcerting. Besides that, her reactions to him overwhelmed her.

He surprised her by eating his burger in under six seconds flat. Mark didn't behave like a pig or anything like that. He looked civilized but manly. Yet, he chewed his burger faster than it took her to recollect her thoughts.

Busy to watch him, she forgot about her food, and he raised his left brow inquiringly, pointing his chin to her plate. She picked up her burger and took a bite. She chewed slowly to gain time and reassess the situation.

She nibbled at her food. However, she focused on the man. Mark looked perfect from a distance. Now, up-close, she could see other things. He had had his nose broken in the past and more than once. A scar divided his right brow into two unequal thick pieces. Another deep line dented his chin and made him look stubborn.

Ella found him fascinating. Some tiny inconsistencies in his behaviour puzzled her, though.

At first sight, Mark looked like the living nightmare of any high-school girl's mother. He was that bad boy, who drove a bike, wore leather jackets, and was always called to the principal's office.

Ella used to dream about those guys in high school, but they never paid an ounce of attention to her. A nerd, she ran with a different crowd.

However, the man's choice of spending the evening with her was out of character. And he even tried to persuade her to dance with him.

Ella assumed that the bad-boy image was just a fabrication. His general behaviour and the polite, albeit fast-eating, proved that he was far from the impression he wanted to give.

MR. RIGHT

Ella didn't always want to be correct, though it would have been nice, at least once in a blue moon. Yet, she was annoyed when she couldn't say what was what. She couldn't read Mark accurately, and that frustrated her.

Mark noticed that she was trying to read him, and an ironic grin flourished on his lips. *'Good luck, pretty woman,'* he thought, and not without some sarcasm. The man didn't mind her efforts to label him. He was sure that she couldn't place him under one of the regular labels women used to classify the men they dated. He wasn't easily classifiable.

Not anymore. Mark could play any role he chose. He didn't want to become a target in someone's plot again. He had learned the hard way not to make it easy for women to read him.

Now Mark was a master at disguising his true colours, a chameleon, and he intended to stay that way. He had found out what Gina saw in him four years ago but still felt the stung, although he had jumped from one woman to another ever since.

He had learned that being open early in a relationship wasn't a good thing. Gina had almost reeled him in, and he had played right in her greedy little hands. He had been hooked, ready to go to the altar.

Still, Mark had been lucky to overhear her plans before that happened. Gina wanted to marry him and make his life a living hell for a few months, so he would ask for a divorce and give her at least half of his fortune. Mark had been blind at the time and hadn't requested Gina to sign a prenup. He hadn't even loved her, and that bothered him more. Her attention had just flattered him.

Now he wanted a bit of fun and taste life on his terms. He didn't have to get married and have kids right away.

Mark was playing the field almost every night. He would go only on a couple of dates with the same woman. Maybe three of four if he was interested enough. The extent of his relationships stretched to a month.

He didn't look for a woman to offer her that happy ever after. He didn't believe in that anymore and wanted to enjoy a few laughs, and if possible, some great sex.

Mark thought that he would have an exciting evening with Ella. She was funny, intelligent, and outspoken. He wasn't very sure about sex, though. Still, he would try.

Mark attacked his cake and watched Ella eating her burger slowly. She assessed him carefully with intelligent eyes, and he enjoyed the show.

He might have looked only for fun, but he had found out that he couldn't have fun with a woman who wasn't smart enough. There wasn't any challenge in that sort of conquest, and he always loved a good challenge.

CHAPTER SIX

ELLA FINALLY POLISHED her dessert, and Mark took her hand to lead her onto the dance floor. Another steamy blues filled the air. The man could smell the intensity of the desire rising in the people dancing on the floor. The melody insinuated in his blood as well.

Mark took Ella in his arms and pulled her closer. The shock rolled through his body at her touch, and he blinked. He had never felt anything so powerful. The connection between the two of them was scary. It was like his body recognized hers at a primitive level.

Although scared, he needed to align their bodies perfectly so that he could taste that unprecedented experience and milk it at maximum.

Ella wrapped her arms around the man's neck and let her body follow his moves. Mark was at least one foot taller than she was, and her head was resting on his chest. He could see the top of her head and smell the fresh scent of her shampoo.

For a few moments, they danced slowly, trying to find a balance between them. Then, Mark brought her even closer. He aligned his pelvis with hers, and she gasped softly. She lost the rhythm for a few seconds, and he grinned.

"Do we have to be so close?" she whispered, looking up at him.

The man answered her question by moving his lower body closer to her. Her eyes got rounder, and a frisson crossed her entire body. Mark relished the faint blush of her skin and just grinned at her.

'Not bad for a former goody two shoe guy,' he thought, proud of himself. Then he lowered his head to kiss her lips and taste her.

She noticed that he lowered his head, and understanding dawned in Ella's short-circuited brain. He would kiss her, and she didn't know what to do. He was moving too fast and too soon for her.

Ella was bright and realistic enough to understand his intentions then. He merely wanted a one-night stand. However, she didn't know if she could do it or not. She wasn't even sure whether she wanted to do it, no matter how attractive he was.

She was far from being a prude, but she had always needed to know the man with whom she would share the sheets. Moreover, she needed to feel something for that man.

Sex was good for health, especially if it was good sex. Nonetheless, sex to scratch an itch wasn't for her. She doubted that she could have sex with Mark just for the sake of sex. Besides, succumbing to a guy's charm within minutes wouldn't have helped her long-term plans.

Ella hadn't made love in a long while, and Mark's body made her feel a lot of things she hadn't felt for some time. She was all knots inside, but that didn't mean she would give him what he wanted, at least not that night.

The man tempted her, so Ella did her best to steel her resolution. She drew back an inch or so as he held her tight in his arms. The young woman looked up at him, looking for the best words to make him understand what she wanted to say without offending him. She thought with regret that she would have liked a second date with him.

"You're good at dancing, Mark. I'll give you that. And you're good at talking, as well. I'm sure you know it, and you don't need me to tell you that. I was just wondering if you were Irish. You got me a few times, so it's fun. Not boring at all. I'd love to spend this night talking and laughing with you. I'd love to get to know you a little better. But you know that's the only thing happening tonight, don't you?" she said with slight hesitation as if she were afraid of his answer.

He held her gaze for a few seconds. She couldn't read anything in his eyes and didn't know if he was disappointed or he agreed with her invitation. Suddenly, that naughty grin came back on his lips. Mark leaned and kissed her briefly. His lips brushed hers for a second, and then, they were gone.

However, a second was what it took. The nerves in Ella's lips twitched and shot arrows of desire through her body. Her breasts ached, and her belly quivered, asking for something more. Her will withered for a moment, but she couldn't go down that path.

Meaningless sex was just that. Meaningless. Ella did need to know him better before giving in to her desires. She also had to stick to her plan if she wanted her life on the right path. Having a one-night stand wouldn't have helped her goals.

Ella leaned her forehead back on his chest. It felt good like she could rely on him. He seemed a strong man.

Mark wouldn't come home whining because his partner had developed his patient base sooner, and he was left behind. He wouldn't complain that he was late for his first appointment, and Mrs. Adams had left before he got there. He wouldn't whine that his car was in service, and he had to take the subway in the morning.

Ella pushed those thoughts aside. Colin wasn't part of her life anymore, and she didn't want to waste any thoughts or time on him.

They danced to another dance in silence. Still, Mark brushed his hand on her back. Sometimes, Ella felt his lips on the top of her head.

She pretended not to feel so that she didn't have to talk about it. It was pure torture to keep her legs moving in the song's rhythm. It was sweet but also hard to resist. She was obsessed with people's hands, and she had the feeling that Mark's hands would feel good on her skin.

Ella argued with herself a little more. She had to listen to the voice in her head that told her not to hurry, so she clung to her beliefs.

After two more slow dances, the band attacked a fast one, and Ella decided that she had danced enough, and they should go back to their table. However, Mark had a different idea, and squeezing her hand, he twirled her around.

Now, Ella panicked. She had never danced a fast dance with someone. She had two left feet when it came to something more than one step to the right, maybe two to the left. That was the sum of her experience.

Ella had tried to learn to waltz when her older sister got married and insisted on having a waltz at the wedding reception. She had expected everyone to dance that waltz.

After the first three lessons, Ella's dance instructor admitted defeat in his twenty-five years of teaching for the first time. Ella just wasn't good at that. She didn't feel the rhythm, and her legs got stiff whenever she tried to dance something other than a slow dance.

Ella loved dancing. She had even entertained some wishful dreaming of becoming a ballerina when she was ten. In the end, she had to accept that she might have many talents but not that one.

Dancing wasn't for her, and she freaked out now. Mark seemed determined to make her dance on the fast rhythm of a rock and roll.

Ella tried to pull her hand back. She wanted to return to the table with her dignity intact. She even managed to say 'no,' but the decibel level went higher, and Mark didn't hear her, or he feigned that he didn't.

Then, he slipped his right arm around her and closed the space between them, leading her around. Ella resigned and tried her best to follow his lead.

Mark leaned to her and whispered in her ear. "Quit being so tense, and just let the rhythm guide your steps, Ella."

"Huh, it's easy for you to say that. I've never danced on something so fast," the woman replied peevishly. Then she skipped a step and missed her footing. She dived directly in Mark's chest.

Mark tightened his arm around her, twirled her to the right, and whispered, "Listen to the music, Ella. Stop thinking of your feet! You'll see that you can do it."

Ella doubted that but didn't bother to contradict him. She needed to concentrate on her moves. Mark would see the error of his words soon enough. She would lose her balance and fall, bringing him down with her. That dance instructor had qualified her as a calamity waiting to happen, and she agreed with him.

Not every day, being a dance instructor would end up on the list of dangerous jobs. The poor man had broken his arm, trying to teach Ella.

Still, one good thing came out of that. The man convinced her sister that it would be classier to keep the waltz for herself and her husband. Then everyone would witness their love.

Her sister loved the idea, so Ella didn't have to dance anymore.

Mark's steel arm moved her expertly while he kept talking to her. She was as stiff as a board and rigid to move initially. However, Mark made her laugh, and soon, she forgot all about dancing, so he didn't need too much effort to lead her. When the dance ended, he grinned at her.

"You see? You can dance if you don't think about your steps."

Stunned, Ella didn't reply. The dance had ended without incident. That man was a witch.

She shrugged and replied, "Well, that's an exception to each rule, you know. I did dance now, but it doesn't mean I could dance again."

He shook his head in disbelief at her stubbornness and led her to their table. They had barely taken their seats to catch their breath when the waitress came to their table.

"Do you want anything else?"

Mark looked at Ella inquiringly, and she nodded.

"Yes, I'd like a coke. But bring the bottle directly to the table, please. I don't need a glass," she said, remembering that she had angered the woman before and fearing the consequences.

"Good thinking," Mark approved. "I'd like a coke, too. Regular, no diet. Right?" he turned to Ella.

"Of course, regular. I can't stand the taste of diet. Too sweet, I think," Ella replied.

"So, just bring the bottles here, please," Mark smiled at the waitress.

The woman immediately forgot to slouch. She showed them that she had quite a fine figure when she made a perfect turn on the tips of her toes.

She left sashaying, and Mark shook his head, a smile forgotten in the corner of his mouth.

"I think we won't have problems with the service for the moment," he said to Ella. "Feel free to come with the coup de grace after we get our drinks," he added, winking at her.

"What's the point?" she shrugged with indifference. "I don't care if she thinks that she's better than I am."

"Good thinking," Mark approved. "It's not like she is anyway, so you shouldn't bother."

Ella smiled at him. His voice seemed sincere enough, and she appreciated the boost. Colin had never gone out of his way to make her feel better.

She knew that Mark had a hidden agenda. She wasn't a naïve teenager. She didn't dream of a knight on a white horse coming to rescue her from a life of total boredom. Yet, his words didn't sound trite.

Ella knew to read people. She dealt with lots of people in her line of work and had already learned the telling signs of lying. She sometimes chose to overlook a lie, but she didn't believe that all people were honest and kind.

"So, you can dance after all," Mark said, leaning toward her, his lips always arched in that grin that she associated with him. "I told you so," he said, patting her hand. "You just need to focus less on dancing and more on something else."

His grin turned naughty, and she guessed his thoughts. He had tried to arouse her when they danced. She didn't even remember that she danced. She couldn't focus on anything but on what was going on under her skin.

"Yeah, you're good at making a woman concentrate on something else," she mumbled.

Nevertheless, Mark heard her and burst into laughter. "Come on, Ella, don't play coy. You liked it. Admit it. I enjoyed it big time. I think we should have a cup of coffee. My place, or yours?" he asked, hoping that she would invite him to her place.

Anyways, if she preferred to go to his place, the man had the perfect way out of that. Mark never brought women home. If he went to their house, he could leave whenever he wanted, and if he didn't want to call them, they couldn't bother him.

Ella captivated him. She seemed intriguing. Still, that wasn't enough to make him forget about his big plan.

Mark had planned to enjoy his playboy-like life for a few years before looking for something more – if he would even start looking for something more in a relationship!

Once stuck in a fake relationship, the man felt the need to spread his wings and have fun. Family life might have been his goal once but represented shackles for a man who cherished his freedom.

He liked Ella enough for a date or two, maybe even a month, but he didn't want to go too far with her. He would be moving on soon, looking for someone else. He didn't need a strong connection, even if he experienced it with Ella right then.

As he was lost in his thoughts, Ella's voice startled him.

"All right, we can have coffee at my place, but only if you understand right now that coffee is not a euphemism for something else," she pointed out. She didn't want any misunderstanding.

"No problem, I was thinking only about coffee," he replied smoothly.

Mark didn't have a problem with her conditions. He had noticed how her body reacted to his, and he knew all the right moves to make her forget about her principles or whatever she had in mind. He believed that he would make her change her mind once they got alone.

After he broke up with Gina, one of his partners offered him a crash course in charming a woman's pants off. Taking that course was the best decision he had ever made. Before that, he had problems getting a woman's attention. Now, he had difficulties making women let him go.

When Ella and Mark stood up to leave, one of the couples they had seen dancing on the floor earlier came to them.

"What would you say if we swung tonight?" the man asked.

His question rendered Ella speechless. No one had ever asked her that. Wide-eyed, she merely stared at Mark, unable to formulate a coherent thought. Her shaking hand was trying to find support on the table.

"We'd like to," the woman purred, her long nails tracing Mark's biceps.

Mark moved slightly off her path and replied in an implacable tone of voice, "No, thanks."

"Come on, man, you two are exactly what we're looking for," the man pleaded.

"Some other time," Mark replied, taking Ella's hand in his.

With a curt nod to the two people, he steered her toward the exit of the club. Mark had noticed that Ella was overwhelmed and unable to react, and he didn't want to waste his time in a dispute with the couple.

By the time they got to the parking lot, Ella had recovered her voice and turned to him. "Oh, my God, I've never had such a ... proposition."

"Then you haven't been in clubs or bars for some time," Mark replied in a dry tone of voice. "It's not so unexpected."

CHAPTER SEVEN

MARK LED ELLA OUT OF the bar, holding her hand as if he were afraid that she would split and run away. The couple's proposition had shocked her, and Mark thought that he shouldn't let go of her hand just yet. He wanted to explore where their acquaintance could go.

Outside the club, the air was crisp, and Mark drew a deep breath. Then he turned to Ella to ask her if she wanted to ride with him in his car, but his eyes fell on the deep frown between the woman's eyebrows. "What's wrong?"

Ella just kept looking at him for a few moments. She assessed him with clinical detachment, although she bit her lips at the same time. She wanted to say something, but she hesitated.

"Come on, Ella, whatever you want to say, just say it," he nudged her, pulling her hand playfully to defuse the situation.

Something bothered her, and he had a good guess about what that might be.

She looked away for a second or two, somewhere in the general direction of the parking lot, and then gazed back at him. Now, she looked square in his eyes.

"Do you do that often?" she asked, afraid of his answer.

"What?" Mark asked, and Ella almost believed he didn't understand her question.

"That swinging thing..." she specified, this time looking down at first and then turning her eyes back to him.

"Ah, that... I had only two choices, Ella, either to say what I said or to plant my fist in that perfect nose of his. By the way, have you noticed that he had it fixed? Anyways, I didn't think you'd like to be involved in a scuffle so...," he said, shrugging and letting her fill in the dots.

Ella kept staring at him, trying to discern whether he was lying. She was afraid of making another wrong choice with a man. Mark merely stared at her. He looked unruffled, and his eyes didn't show his thoughts.

Ella thought she would see what kind of man he was soon enough, so she nodded.

"So, do you want me to follow you home or ...?" Mark asked.

"I don't think I want to leave my car here over the night. I drank non-alcoholic beer, so I think I'd better take my car, and you can follow me," Ella said. She was thankful that Jo wasn't there anymore to lecture her and that she could drive her car back home.

"So, where did you park?" Mark asked her.

She showed him a spot at the far end of the parking lot, and he decided to see her in her car. There wasn't much light in that spot, and he wasn't willing to take unnecessary risks for a few minutes of walking.

Everyone knew what happened in such areas late at night, especially when a woman was alone. Once he heard the click of the lock, Mark jogged to his car to follow her home. He wouldn't have liked to see Ella become a statistic in a police report.

Ella took the time to think of him and a possible relationship with him during her drive home.

She was smart enough to understand that he expected to change her mind and spend part of the night with her. Still, she was strong enough not to yield to those troubling green eyes, shadowed by the blackest eyelashes she had ever seen. Mark could mesmerize her just by staring at her, and that wouldn't do at all.

She also had to consider that he might insist. But then, she was confident in her ability to fight off any unwanted advances if he would become too enthusiastic and didn't understand the word no.

Ella counted on her four years of training in a dojo downtown. Even though she hadn't been there in more than a month, she still knew her moves. Bryan had taught her everything she needed to take care of herself.

ELLA STOPPED IN FRONT of her building. Lowering her window, she showed Mark where to find the visitors' parking lot, and then, she drove to her parking spot.

They met again in front of the door leading into the building, and she used her card key to let him inside, where she greeted the concierge.

"Hi, Tom, you've got the late shift again, I see."

"Yes, ma'am. Dean had to go away for two days, and I needed the hours," the old man said with a shrug.

Ella knew what he meant. Surviving in Toronto meant a lot of work and sacrifice.

"He's my friend, Mark," Ella explained to him when Tom's eyes stopped on Mark, scrutinizing the younger man.

Tom nodded and looked after them when they went to the south elevators to the 24th floor.

"I suppose you have a great view from up there," Mark observed when she pushed the button for the floor.

"Yep, the best," she agreed, proud of her condo. "That's why I bought this condo. I know it isn't large. It's got only two bedrooms. However, my balcony overlooks the harbour. The view is fantastic. Most of the summer, I spend it out there," she replied, smiling at him with warmth. "I'd sleep there if I could, but I'm not that crazy yet," she continued and laughed nervously.

Mark smiled and nodded. However, he finally accepted the truth. It was clear that he hadn't made a wise choice for that evening, although he liked the young woman a lot. She seemed unspoiled and bright, and she looked gorgeous, precisely what he fancied.

Her self-assurance in the bar at the beginning of the evening made him believe that she played hard to get. Now he had his doubts. It was evident that Ella didn't bring men home for one night of wild fun, and that was his purpose for the moment.

Her home was genuinely warm. The paintings on the walls featured trees at the beginning of fall, trails covered with rusty leaves, and foggy parks basking in the grey light of late fall. The colours followed the autumn palette of the auburn carpet.

Everything around revealed that the woman was a romantic at heart. She might have felt alone sometimes, separated from the world, but she also enjoyed her solitude at times.

Mark's hopes plummeted now. Ella wasn't the merry type he had initially thought. She didn't play with him when she told him that her invitation didn't involve anything else but coffee.

He needed to make his exit soon. He wasn't there for the long run and didn't intend to change that.

She showed him on the balcony, where the breeze of the lake tamed the heat of the day. The smell of water and weeds reached them even on the 24th floor.

Ella left him there to admire the panorama of the harbour and went to make the coffee she had promised. She also arranged a platter with the small coffee cakes she had baked the day before.

When she returned to him, his eyes gleamed at the sight of her cakes. She was happy whenever someone appreciated her baking.

Ella liked cooking and baking. That was the sum of her likes when it came to housework. Everything else was just a necessity, not a pleasure.

"Here you are," she said, putting a cup and saucer in front of him on the little square table she had set on her balcony.

Then, she arranged the platter with coffee cakes, the sugar bowl, and milk. Ella poured his coffee first, and then she filled her cup, adding some sugar and milk.

She felt Mark's eyes on her hands and felt like she was playing in a theatre play in front of an audience. That was just a little unnerving for her unsteady nerves.

She knew her hands lacked the grace her mother had tried to teach her. Of course, her mother had failed. Ella preferred playing soccer or basketball and refused to learn serving tea etiquette.

Ella's mother came from a middle-class environment and married in the middle class. However, she had hoped that her daughters might elevate their social status.

She did her best to prepare them and succeeded with Ella's sister. To her joy, her daughter snagged a mogul, as she liked to say.

But Ella disappointed her. She didn't socialize with people simply because they had money and belonged to a specific class.

Now, noticing Mark's critical eyes on her busy hands, Ella had a fleeting moment of regret. She should have learned the art of serving tea, as well. It wouldn't have been as if she had sold her soul. It was only a skill to show off.

Mark stilled her hands with one of his. "Everything's perfect, Ella. Just have your coffee, and let's talk a little."

Ella blushed. She had fussed over everything like a young housewife over the first visit to her house, and now she felt embarrassed.

Noticing a few sails at the horizon, Mark started chatting about boats and asked her how she felt about sailing. She watched a plane landing on the strip on the island, and then she shrugged.

"I don't know. Of course, I went on a three-hour cruise, and I've always promised myself I'd take a cruise in the Caribbean, but you know how it is. It's never the right moment. Always something else comes up," Ella said, sipping from her coffee. "Maybe one day, I'll go."

"I love sailing," Mark confessed and bit into one of the cakes. "These are heavenly," he exclaimed, and Ella smiled at him, satisfied that at least there she did well.

"You said you liked sailing," Ella started and took a cake, too. "Do you own a boat?" she asked curiously.

"No, I don't," Mark lied without blinking. "I'm lucky enough to have friends who do, though," he said, winking at her and making her burst into laughter. "So, now and then, I have a chance to go out on the lake. I haven't taken a cruise in the Caribbean yet, but I intend to rectify this error sometime in winter. You know what I mean. I'll need to get rid of the harshness of the climate here and stretch on the hot sand, holding one of those drinks with tiny umbrellas...."

"It's not so bad in winter," Ella replied, leaning back and crossing her legs.

Mark noticed the patch of skin under the hem of the dress and decided he had to try his luck, no matter what. That woman made him want her. She had crawled under his skin.

He leaned toward her and nonchalantly laid his palm on her knee, whispering, "Wouldn't we be more comfortable inside, for example, on your sofa, Ella?"

For a moment there, Ella hesitated. The roughened skin on her unclad leg made her feel disturbing things. However, she made an effort and pushed them at the back of her mind. She wasn't a prude, not by far, but she knew she would hate herself in the morning if she didn't get to know him better before letting their relationship advance at the speed of light.

"Here or there, it's the same thing, Mark. I've already told you we'd drink some coffee and talk. I hoped you understood," she replied in a clipped tone of voice.

A metallic shine appeared in his green eyes at her tone, and he assessed her methodically. The cynical light in his eyes chilled her to the bones.

"All right, I get it. I enjoyed your company. Well, the coffee was great; the cakes excellent. Anyway, I'd better leave now," Mark said. His cold voice sent chills down her spine. "I'm not into playing games, Ella. High school is way behind me."

Ella frowned for a second, but then she just let it go. She understood Mark's goal was to score, and she didn't matter in the big scheme of things. Anybody would do it for him. Although she hadn't fallen for him, she felt cheap and used, but, at least, he hadn't scored.

Like in an ice-cold trance, Ella stood up. She said in an indifferent voice, "Then don't let me hold you any longer, Mark. You know where the door is, don't you?" she waved toward the living room so that he would understand that she wanted him to leave.

Mark looked at her for a few seconds, and then, nodding, he stood as well, going to the front door. He stopped a moment there, seemed to think of something, and then, he turned to her.

Ella was still at the door of the balcony, her cold gaze following his progress through her house.

Mark couldn't read anything in her eyes. He hesitated for a moment, and then, even though he didn't know why, he said, "It isn't personal, you know. You're a great woman, Ella, but...."

"Yeah, I know. I'm a great woman, the coffee was great as well as the cake, and you didn't get what you wanted. So, what are you waiting for?" she asked, nodding to the door, completely fed up with egotistic males for one day.

He shook his head and went out of her house and life in silence. Ella didn't move for several minutes. Then she slowly sat down, took a slice of cake off the platter, and started mincing it unconsciously.

Her mind refused to register any thought but simply took in the scent of the night and the splendour of the harbour.

That day went into the column with wasted opportunities. She had gone out to grab a new future, and that future crumbled at her feet. Well, there was always tomorrow. She had to go on.

CHAPTER EIGHT

THAT WAS THE SECOND evening in a row when Mark couldn't find what he was looking for, and his frustration only grew more. He had been cruising the bars for the last two evenings, and he even went into two clubs but left disappointed.

Ella's image was always there, at the back of his mind. Mark couldn't focus on another woman, although he spoke to a few. He either didn't like the sound of their voice or the colour of their eyes.

Anyway, regardless of why, he didn't enjoy the time spent with them. He bought them a couple of drinks, spent about ten or fifteen minutes with each of them, and then left to look elsewhere.

Leaving the last bar he visited, Mark stopped outside and fidgeted with his watch. Dissatisfaction was gnawing at him. More concerning, though, his weakness annoyed him. Yet, he knew he had to do something about his obsession with that woman. He had spent a few hours with Ella during a Friday night, and now, he couldn't find any joy in the chase. That spelled trouble for him.

He needed to have Ella. It was as simple as that. Mark was sure that he would be able to move on once he had had a few nights with her, maybe even just one.

Those days, he would get bored with women fast. They had become interchangeable, and he didn't see any reason to stick around when his interest waned.

Mark checked his watch once more, noticing that it was already past nine. He oscillated between waiting until the next day but put the thought aside. He knew that he wouldn't get a chance to get laid that night, but he longed to hear her voice at least.

He decided to cultivate their relationship and date her a few times so that he could finally get her in his bed. Mark didn't understand why he needed her so badly and why he couldn't hook up with another woman, but he was a rational man and never fought windmills. He always did what he had to do to get from point A to B.

The drive to the harbour was easy enough. The traffic wasn't bad for a Sunday evening, and Mark cruised easily.

He was uncomfortable with the churning inside him. He upped the volume of the cd-player, hoping that music would help dissipate the strange trepidation drumming in his gut.

He couldn't wait to lay his eyes on Ella, although he was afraid of what she would say about his visit. He doubted she would be happy to see him, but he counted on his inherent charm to sway her anger around.

The problem was gaining entrance into the building because he had to pass by the concierge.

Philosophically, he shrugged. He would see once he got there.

Mark decided to leave his car in a parking lot close to the building because he didn't want to discuss the parking problem with the concierge.

At the entrance in the building, he was lucky enough because a couple went inside. He rushed his steps so that he didn't have to wait outside until Ella would make up her mind to allow him inside.

Once in the lobby, he started toward the front desk, but luck was on his side again. The concierge wasn't there. In a way, Mark loved a good sign. It meant that he had the green light in his quest, and he never said no when chance knocked on the door.

Mark changed direction to the south elevators, rubbing his hands with glee. He knew it would be easier to convince Ella to let him in her condo if he didn't have to plead his case through a third party.

The couple that came in before took the same elevator, so he managed to pass through the second set of doors without problems.

Mark got out of the elevator and suddenly stopped. The thought that she might not be alone at that hour popped into his mind for the first time, and he frowned. He was one of the most methodical guys on earth, and he hadn't considered all possible scenarios. That wasn't like him at all.

Mark hesitated for a second, and then, decisively, he strode to her door and knocked. He didn't want to give himself the time to change his mind.

"Who's there?" he heard her shaky voice from inside.

Probably, no one came upstairs without being announced by the concierge downstairs beforehand and without her okay.

"Mark," he answered and listened to the quietness that followed and enveloped everything. He couldn't hear steps or anything coming from inside her apartment. The insulation of those condos seemed very good.

Mark didn't even know if Ella was still in the hall or if she went out on her cherished balcony. She might have gone into her bedroom, leaving him hanging in the corridor.

Seconds passed, but it felt like minutes to him. When the lock clicked, he breathed deeply. The door opened, and Ella appeared on the threshold.

He grinned, displaying his white and regular teeth. He had seen a beautifully composed woman dressed for the kill the other day. Now his gaze fell on the woman in her more private moments.

Ella's mussed short hair looked like she had played with her fingers through it. Her shorts and tank top didn't hide any of her curves. She didn't wear any makeup, and her skin appeared paler, contrasting even more with her black eyes and shiny dark hair.

Mark saw a good deal of skin, and his eyes zeroed in on her breasts. They stretched the top, trying to escape their confinement. She didn't have a bra on, which made his blood get hotter. He was already primed as he had thought of her during the entire ride there.

With a hand on the door, Ella just stared at him for a few moments and fidgeted uncomfortably under his searching eyes. She had noticed that his eyes fell on the top of her breasts, and she regretted that she hadn't put a bra on that evening.

"So, why the honour of your visit?" she attacked him.

"I needed to see you... talk to you," Mark answered, looking up, his eyes on hers now.

"I thought you didn't have time to play stupid games," Ella retorted and not without some malice. She could be mean when she had to. She wasn't a shrinking violet.

"Well, I've been wrong," he admitted in an even tone of voice. "I'd like to know you better... spend some time with you...."

'Yeah, sure...' she thought. She didn't believe Mark for a second.

"You haven't found anyone to score with tonight, that's it?" she asked, knowing very well that she sounded like a shrew, but she didn't care.

She had already deleted his name from her list. *'As if you had a list!'* she chided herself bitterly.

After the fiasco with Mark on Friday, she didn't repeat the escapade on Saturday or Sunday but spent all the time by herself. She needed to recover from her first defeat and gather the courage to go out again.

"I haven't come here to score, Ella," Mark answered in a calm tone of voice, hoping that she would be more sympathetic if he didn't attack back.

He was honest enough to admit that he deserved her bitterness. He also knew that she might get even angrier by the end of their brief relationship. Yet, he was willing to take that risk to get what he wanted.

"How did you pass by the concierge?" Ella inquired, not very little surprised that he had come right up to her apartment.

She knew that the concierge wasn't the man to swallow any sappy story, especially if his job was on the line.

"He wasn't there," Mark said and shrugged. "A couple came into the building, and I followed them. Will you continue to interrogate me here on the hall all night, or will you invite me inside?" he asked her, trying to sound playful.

"Nothing changed," she said curtly.

"I didn't think it did," Mark replied. "But, I realized that I wanted to know you better, and I understand that you need time to know me as well, so... Here I am," he grinned again.

Mark saw that Ella considered his words carefully.

On Friday evening, she had proved that she was brilliant. She wouldn't lie to herself and believe that he was there because he had suddenly fallen in love with her and couldn't live without her. She was cynical enough to think that he hadn't forgotten about scoring with her.

He could read her thoughts on her face, after all. It was like he was inside her brain. That was refreshing. He was sick of always trying to be one step ahead and guess what women were thinking.

Mark knew that Ella was aware that she might set herself up for disappointment in the end if she allowed him back in her life.

She waved him inside, and he mentally gave himself a high five, releasing a sigh of relief. He had been half afraid that her common sense might prevail, and she might close the door right in his nose without even talking to him.

Ella led the way to the balcony, where she had left a carafe with lemonade and a plate with the cookies she had baked earlier that day. Whenever she was agitated, she would bake, although she worried about her hips.

She invited him to take a seat and asked, "Would you like some lemonade or something else? I'm pretty sure I have some whiskey in the house and probably also some non-alcoholic beer."

"Lemonade's fine with me," Mark answered. He had already drunk a few beers that day, and he still had to drive back home later that evening.

Ella nodded and went inside to bring him a glass. His eyes burnt the skin on her back, and the feeling was disconcerting.

She didn't know whether she had made the right choice letting him in her house, and subsequently in her life, even if for only a few hours. She would have time for regrets later. But she felt alone that evening, and she welcomed some companionship.

After the night when she asked him to leave, she didn't find the courage to go hunting again, especially after answering Jo's questions on Saturday morning.

Ella didn't tell Jo what exactly happened with Mark. She didn't want to hear any 'I told you so' during the many years to come. If she knew Jo, and she did, Jo was able to remind her of that fiasco even on her death bed.

Returning with a glass for him, Ella poured him a glass of lemonade and rearranged the plate and napkins on the table so that he could reach them easily. She needed time to pull herself together.

She avoided looking at him. She didn't know how to behave with a man like him.

Mark was the first man to tell her that he was interested only in a relationship with benefits. At least, he hadn't lied, and that was a good point for him. The truth hurt, but she preferred it at any time.

Mark touched her right hand gently and stilled her moves. It felt like a déjà-vu.

"Ella, it's fine. You shouldn't worry. We'll have some lemonade and cakes, and we'll talk. Maybe we'll watch a movie together. I won't ask for more than that."

Ella looked up at him, judging his attitude. She didn't know if he had lied. However, she was willing to give him the benefit of the doubt.

After a long time spent with Colin, who lied all the time, she could spend an evening with another man, even if that evening wouldn't lead to anything.

CHAPTER NINE

ELLA BRUSHED HER HAIR with rushed movements and then watched herself in the mirror. She looked good. Well, as good as possible after a long day at work.

She had had so much to do during the last couple of days that she almost lacked the energy to go out. The dark circles around her eyes bore witness to her exhaustion and painted her skin with shadows.

She knew that although she was tired, she would still go out. Mark had spent almost every evening with her during the last three weeks, and she had enjoyed his company.

He was a good conversationalist, witty, and even sarcastic when necessary. More important, he wasn't dull. Every time they got together, she was fascinated with his ideas, and the time seemed to move fast. He didn't push to move their relationship in a specific direction, and that was both interesting and unexpected.

Mark had a lot of imagination and surprised Ella all the time. She never knew what to expect from him, and he never told her what he had planned.

Probably, that was why she was never tired of him. Always something new happened, and even if they spent time over a meal or watching a movie, the conversation was sparkling.

There was also that electrical spark between them that made her skin tingle and put crazy ideas in her head. However, Ella didn't know whether Mark felt it, as well, and she didn't want to ask him.

She was afraid. Attacking that subject head-on might have brought an unwanted change in their relationship. For the time being, she liked the status-quo, although she knew it was only temporary.

Ella was painfully aware of what Mark wanted. He had never made a secret of that. He tried not to deceive her, which was remarkable, albeit unsettling.

Mark was careful and never said anything she could have construed as a love declaration. Ella had expected that from him initially, and his behaviour puzzled her. He didn't make her believe that he was interested in a serious and long-term relationship with her either.

Ella knew that he enjoyed spending time with her. Otherwise, he wouldn't have kept showing up unexpectedly or calling her every day. Yet, that didn't mean that Mark had lost sight of his initial purpose. He took every chance to touch her and drive her crazy.

His fingers would brush over her hand, or he would put his hand at the small of her back when they would go into an establishment. He would dance with her and hold her tight in his arms. Their bodies would rub one to the other, and arousal would hum in her blood and demand fulfillment. It felt like torture, sweet, but still, torture.

In other words, Mark drove her crazy. He enjoyed seeing her off balance, and Ella was tense all the time. Every fibre in her body was screaming for release, and she knew that she was ready to capitulate soon.

At least now, Ella knew the man beyond those mocking and undecipherable eyes. She also had to admit that she liked him a lot. Maybe, it was time to let their relationship evolve or die of natural causes. At least, she'd feel good in the process.

Ella didn't know whether Mark would disappear from her life once he had made love to her, but maybe it was high time to find out.

She wanted him anyway, and she was willing to take the risk, even if that would bring her just a certain measure of peace.

One thing bothered her, though. They would always spend time at her house or outside, but Mark never invited her to his place. That troubled her. It was as if he hadn't wanted to let Ella know too much about him or step into the most important corners of his life. Even that evening, Mark came to take her out for dinner. Ella didn't think that dinner would be at his place.

Ella glanced at her watch and grimaced. Mark would be downstairs in about ten minutes. It was almost time to meet him. She glanced at herself in the mirror once more and then gathered her things.

She left the washroom and passed by the empty reception desk. Marge, the receptionist, had already left like everybody else on the floor. Maybe only one of the partners, Mr. Phileas, was still in his office at that hour.

Everybody else had already gone home or somewhere else for drinks to shake off the tension of the demanding work. However, Mr. Phileas was well known for his long work hours, especially when he had a court appearance the following day.

Ella took the elevator downstairs, and passing by the front desk, she went out of the building. The security guard must have been on one of his rounds because no one was at the front desk.

After leaving the building, she glanced right and then left. Mark wasn't anywhere in sight, so she went toward the parking lot around the corner. She was supposed to meet Mark there.

Ella remembered a bench just around the corner before getting into the parking. The smokers in the company preferred that spot. She thought to rest there for a few minutes. She had run many errands that day and hadn't spent much time at her desk.

Mark hadn't arrived yet, so she strode to the bench to wait. The light from a lamppost fell over the bench seat, so the place looked safe.

Just two steps away from the bench, hurried steps sounded from behind her, and the hairs at the back of her neck stood up. She turned and noticed that two men had come after her. Their bearing was telling, and Ella's heart started beating furiously. Anxiety spread through her veins.

The evening was warm, yet both men wore hooded jackets, and they had covered their heads. She couldn't catch a glimpse of their features or hair colour, and that scared her even more.

The short man grabbed her handbag. The other grasped her arm and pulled her to him.

Ella had learned to defend herself. She had spent many an evening at a dojo downtown for four years. The woman had learned a lot, even though she hadn't trained for two months. Nonetheless, fear paralyzed her, and she nearly forgot to fight back.

That made it easy for the tall guy. With the advantage on his side for a few seconds, he practically immobilized her just before the fog vanished from her brain, and she started fighting back. She kneed him in his private parts and had the satisfaction to draw a groan out of him.

Her joy had a brief life. She had forgotten about the other one in the heat of the moment. Still, he was there, clenching her handbag. Seeing that the woman had injured his friend, the man roared and planted his fist in her temple. Ella fell to the ground like a sack of potatoes and lost consciousness for a minute or two. Everything went black.

When she finally came around, her eyes fell on Mark. He knocked the two men's heads one to the other and threw the men away as yesterday's garbage.

Ella couldn't shake the impression that she woke up in the middle of a movie. Mark revealed the agility of a ninja. She had seen that kind of move only in films.

The two men shook their heads to clear them and launched back to Mark, only to be welcomed by a skilled fighter. Mark didn't seem to make any effort, although he didn't move gracefully. Mark didn't go for beauty but brutal efficiency. He made every one of his moves count, and the results were staggering.

Ella sat up with effort and winced in pain. She still had some vision trouble. Fog surrounded everything, and she knew for a fact that there was no fog that night. A terrible migraine started to annoy her. Someone with a drum had a good time on her expense somewhere in her head.

She started biting her nails when the two men tried to jump Mark simultaneously. Mark was well built. Yet, two strong strapping men attacked him, and the fight wasn't fair by far, with one against two.

Worried or not, she couldn't stop watching him. Mark's style of fighting was impressive. He used both his fists and legs at the same time.

Watching his precise movements, Ella understood that he wasn't at a disadvantage. He had trained to fight and proved a methodical fighter. He didn't waste effort on anything unless the result was positive. That conclusion made her breathe easier.

When the tall attacker dug out a knife from his jacket, Ella held her breath. The man launched at Mark, holding the blade with the tip down.

Ella tried to stand up, her eyes looking frantically for something around to use against him. She still felt the effects of the blow in her temple and was a little dizzy. She staggered for a few moments, trying to find her balance.

She had just found her legs when a scream reached her ears, and she froze. Her head turned toward the sound, just in time to see the man's arm bent at an unnatural angle. The knife slipped from his fingers, falling on the pavement. A clank that resounded in the almost empty parking. Only Mark's car was there.

Hurried steps came, and afraid that the two attackers received reinforcements, she glanced in the direction of the sound. The security guard was running toward them, speaking into his station radio.

Over the swarm of wasps that had made a nest in her ears and whose buzzing was deafening, Ella couldn't understand what the man was saying.

She already had blurred vision, but now everything became gradually darker, and she fell deep into the black tunnel of unconsciousness.

Ella opened her eyes with difficulty. She still saw stars before her eyes. She didn't wake when Mark slapped her face lightly, but she did at the police siren that filled the evening. The little man with a drum from inside her brain continued playing, and that made her wince. She hated him from all her heart.

Ella became aware that Mark held her in his lap. He had carried her to the bench earlier, and now, he was cradling her in his arms. Mark brushed the hair off her face. He looked into her eyes and saw the signs of a concussion.

"We need to make a trip to the hospital, Ella," he said in a calm and measured tone of voice.

She tried to protest, and he stopped her with a finger on her lips. "No, that's not negotiable, I'm afraid," he continued in an implacable voice. "A doctor must check you. After that, we'll see."

"You still need to give us a statement, sir," a police officer said. "Both of you," he continued, turning to Ella.

Ella and Mark looked up at him. Although the siren had woken her up, Ella didn't realize someone had called the police.

"Of course, officer," Mark replied. "It's not very complicated. I came to take Ella out for dinner. I got here, and I saw those two men attack her," he said, pointing toward the two attackers.

Another police officer was leading the two cuffed men toward the police cruiser. A satisfied grin perched on Mark's lips.

"Anyways, I got here just in time to see Ella knee the big one. Before I could get off the car, the other one planted a fist on the side of her face, and she fell," Mark explained and then stopped to look down at Ella.

He brushed his fingers tenderly over the side of her face, and his lips tightened in a hard line.

"After she fell, that individual started tearing off her clothes, and I intervened," Mark continued, looking back to the officer. "We fought for a few minutes. One of them came with a knife at me, and I'm afraid I broke his arm in the process of defending myself. When I finished with him, I took care of the second guy. I think that's the sum of the events," Mark shrugged.

"Yes, that part with the knife we knew," the officer nodded.

He turned his eyes to the police car to see if his colleague had any problems with the men they had arrested. Then, he turned back to Ella and Mark.

"The security guard told the 911 agent about the knife. He didn't know exactly how everything started because he was doing his rounds. However, when he got back to his station, he saw on the monitor that the lady was fighting the thugs," he explained. "Now, ma'am, could you tell me what happened to you?" the officer turned to Ella.

Ella recounted what had happened before Mark arrived at the scene. She didn't remember anything about her clothes being torn off. Now that she knew about it, she could see that her outfit was ruined.

The police officer took their information to contact them later if necessary and joined his colleague after placing the two attackers in the police car. Only one of them had both hands cuffed. The other one needed medical attention and couldn't use one of his arms anyway.

Mark helped Ella stand up and led her to his car. "Next stop, the emergency room, pretty woman," he said. "If you're good, I'll cook for you tonight," he continued, smiling at her while helping her get into the car.

He took care to fasten her seatbelt, and then, he drove to St. Michael's Hospital, where they spent almost two hours waiting before a doctor could see Ella.

The emergency room was full of people and depressing. Still, despite Ella's complaints, Mark held to his decision to have her checked out. He didn't even want to discuss leaving the hospital before that.

The doctor confirmed Mark's diagnosis. Ella had a concussion and needed rest. He gave her a Tylenol and advised her to avoid any other pain medication for a couple of days.

Mark had insisted on a CAT scan, and he persuaded the doctor to send Ella to a scan. In the end, Mark was satisfied to learn that everything was all right.

He took Ella back to his car. After they left the parking, he glanced at her and noticed that she had closed her eyes and tried to rest, although a line burrowed between her brows.

"As I promised, I'll cook for you tonight. We'll have to stop at a supermarket, though, but you can rest in the car until I finish shopping. I'll be fast, you'll see."

"Okay," Ella answered softly. "Everything is fine with me right now."

Mark smiled, looking at her. Then he shook his head and drove to the closest supermarket. He advised Ella to lock the doors after him and left only after hearing the locks click shut.

Ella closed her eyes and almost fell asleep when Mark returned with several bags full of groceries. She opened her eyes for just enough time to see him getting into the car and then closed them back again.

"WE'RE HERE, ELLA," Mark shook her shoulder, and she woke up with a jerk. Her eyes were wide and scared. "It's just me, don't be scared," Mark whispered and stroked the side of her face.

Ella nodded. Then she noticed he had stopped the car in front of her building. Disappointment tasted bitter on her tongue. It was evident that Mark didn't want her to know where he lived. She would have liked to shout at him, but she didn't feel strong enough to quarrel with him right then, so she just smiled sadly.

"Do you want to park in the visitors' lot or where you always park when you come here?" she asked him.

"I'll leave the car in the visitors' parking tonight. I don't want that you walked a long distance," he replied.

"Don't make me any favours," she bit out. "Park wherever you want. And by the way, you don't have to babysit me. I wouldn't want your night ruined with all of this," she continued sarcastically.

Ella knew that she sounded like a shrew, but she couldn't refrain herself. Mark looked at her for a few seconds, trying to assess her mood.

"I don't think it would ruin my night if I took care of you. Besides, I promised you dinner, and I'm a man of my word," he replied thoughtfully.

"Yeah, sure," she muttered, although she knew that she wasn't fair.

Mark had never told her an outright lie. But then, he systematically avoided bringing her to his house, which was disconcerting.

"Okay, Ella, I understand you've had a rough night, and you have an awful headache," he said in a grave tone of voice. "That's why I won't take it personally. Let's park the damn car and go upstairs."

The man was upset, although he tried to look understanding. Ella glanced at him again. She noticed the lines set at the corners of his mouth. He was annoyed because Ella didn't want his help. Unconcerned, she shrugged. The young woman didn't care about that. She had reasons to be upset with him.

Mark gritted his teeth, and his fingers clenched on the steering wheel. He glanced at her once more and then started the car. He drove to the visitors' parking lot, where he helped her out and gathered the bags he had left in the back seat.

The ride in the elevator was silent and tense. Ella looked down all the time, not to meet his eyes. She could feel Mark's gaze on her. His constant attention felt somewhat unnerving, and her resolve not to talk to him started crumbling. Luckily for her, they got to her floor before she caved in. As soon as they entered the apartment, she went into the bedroom without a word.

CHAPTER TEN

ELLA TOOK OFF THE REMNANTS of her outfit and threw them into the bin in the bathroom. Then she took a shower, and dressed in black sweatpants and a white t-shirt, she went into the living room. Immediately, her gaze fell on Mark. He was busy in the kitchen chopping peppers. Feeling her presence, he glanced at her and smiled.

"Feeling better now?" he inquired.

Ella nodded and walked to the kitchen island. She was barefoot, and the thick carpet covering the floors muffled the sound of her steps.

She sat on the barstool and asked, "Do you need any help?"

"No, don't worry. Everything's under control," Mark replied. "The chicken is almost ready. I merely have to add the vegetables," he said, putting the peppers into the pan and stirring the meat and the vegetables with expert moves. He didn't seem out of place in her kitchen, which surprised her.

It smelled spicy, and Ella felt her mouth water. She had eaten a sandwich at noon, but that had been a while ago. Now, she was famished even though her head was still troubling her.

"I checked the cupboards and took out the plates," Mark said. "Do you want to eat here or in the living room?"

"Here's fine," she answered.

While showering, Ella had decided not to split hairs anymore. If Mark wanted more, that was fine. If not, overthinking wouldn't change that anyway.

She knew she would have to decide what to do soon. Time passed her by, and if she wanted to fulfill her plans, she needed to do something about it. Just waiting wasn't good enough anymore.

Mark dished out the food and poured a glass of orange juice for each. They started dining in silence.

"What upset you, Ella?" "That I wasn't there in time to save you from those thugs or something else?" Mark asked after a few minutes of total silence.

Ella looked up, baffled. "What are you talking about?" she asked.

"I can see you're upset with me. You've been upset all evening. I thought it was because of what happened in the parking lot, but I might be wrong."

She shook her head, "Be serious! It wasn't your fault. And you saved me in the end if you remember," she said, tilting her head. She gazed at him with narrowed eyes. "I think I forgot to thank you," she said pensively, a little ashamed.

He waved her concern away. "You don't have to thank me. Anybody would have done the same thing," he replied.

"Not really," Ella said. "People don't always get in the middle of a scuffle when the odds are against them."

"The odds weren't against me, Ella," Mark replied, baffled. "I can handle two attackers; sometimes, even three. Of course, I'm not always the victor, but hey, only today matters," he said with a chuckle.

"Yeah, you're good, I'll give you that. You've been training for long, haven't you?"

"Yes, I have. I normally train three times a week, at least; sometimes more. It pays, as you could see," he grinned at her with mischief.

"Yes, it does," she agreed, forking some more of her stir-and-fry. "You're good at cooking, too. I'll give you that," she remarked after chewing carefully.

"I'm alone. I'm sick of take-out or eating in town. Cooking's become a priority," Mark answered. "Don't let this fool you, though. I can cook stir-fry and pasta. Of course, I can grill a steak. But nothing else, I'm afraid."

Ella put her fork down and stood up.

"Where are you going?" Mark inquired, also standing up.

"I need some water. I must have some in the pantry," the woman replied.

"You can ask me," Mark said and showed her back to her barstool. "Come on. You have to rest, Ella. Don't forget that you've got a serious concussion, and you shouldn't move around so much," he said, going to the pantry to take the water.

"The doctor didn't say anything of the kind," she replied curtly, and her stubborn voice pricked his ears.

"So what?" he came back with the water and another glass. "I think he thought it was a given, and he didn't have to spell it out for you."

"Really?"

"Yes, really," he said in an authoritative voice, pouring the water in her glass. "And anyway, I'm here, and I can bring you water if you want some. Why go through the trouble if someone else can make it easier for you?"

Ella took the glass and drank. She played with the glass for a few seconds and then put it on the table.

"That's why you're here? To make it easier for me?"

"But of course! What did you think?"

She didn't answer immediately, and he could see that she was giving a lot of consideration to what she was going to say.

"Mark, you were very direct from the beginning. You told me what you wanted from me that very night, you remember?"

"Yes, of course, I do. So? Where's this conversation going, Ella?"

"I was wondering...."

"About what?" Mark asked, sitting down again and tackling his food as if the conversation couldn't make him forget about his dinner.

Ella fidgeted in her seat, but then she met his eyes daringly and said, "What has changed?"

"Changed?" he asked with bafflement. He wasn't sure what the woman wanted to say. "Nothing has changed, Ella. I still want to sleep with you if that's what you're asking. I've just been waiting for you to decide when."

Ella's jaw dropped. She was dumbfounded. She hadn't expected such a direct answer, although she should have known better. Until she processed his words, she stared at him, mouth agape. Then her mouth closed with a clinking of teeth.

"So, that's why you're here now," she concluded.

"Don't be absurd," he replied in an irritated tone. "You aren't fit to have sex right now. I know what my goal is, but I'm not a jackass. Tonight, it's about you getting better. Whether I get you into the sack or not, we'll keep for another time."

Ella had mixed feelings now. She felt exhilarated that he wanted to take care of her because it meant that he did care for her in a certain measure. Yet, she also felt like a piece of merchandise and had the urge to throw him out.

The conflicting feelings and the rush of thoughts worsened her migraine. Instinctively, she started massaging her temples.

"I think you'd better take two Tylenol now and try to get some sleep. I will stay, don't worry. If you need me, just let me know."

Ella glanced at him. She wanted to continue with their discussion, but she gave up. She didn't have the strength for that.

She took the pills from Mark and washed them down with some water. Then she merely left the kitchen and went to her bedroom. Once inside, she carefully closed the door behind her and threw herself on the bed, closing her eyes and praying for the piercing pain to go away.

Mark followed her by sight. He knew she was conflicted and didn't understand what he was saying. He, himself, couldn't make too much sense.

He was on the prowl, as always. Despite that, he also needed to take care of Ella, which bothered him.

It also worried him that he had been pursuing Ella for a few weeks and abandoned his usual game. He had trained himself not to care about women, just to take and leave, and now, he loathed his behaviour.

CHAPTER ELEVEN

ELLA WOKE UP, FEELING the soft touch of Mark's fingers on the side of her face. She opened her eyes. He was near the bed, bending over her. He brushed the hair off her face, a habit of his, and kissed her lips chastely.

"Good morning, sleeping beauty. Just half an hour more, and I could have said good afternoon," Mark grinned at her.

Ella smiled back, but suddenly, she remembered she should have been at work hours ago. She jumped out of bed, slightly missing his head with her shoulder.

"Hey, hey, what are you doing? Where's the damn fire?" Mark asked with bafflement, barely avoiding an elbow in his mouth.

Ella had already leaped out of bed and was running into the bathroom, so she yelled back, "I should have been at work. God, what am I going to do?"

Mark came after her and stopped her from ripping her pyjamas off. "Calm down, Ella. I took care of everything, don't worry. They know what happened to you last night and told me that you should stay home today. Anyway, the security guard had already reported when I called."

Ella stopped suddenly and turned to him in slow motion. She couldn't believe her ears. "You called my office and told them what happened," she repeated as if she weren't sure that she had heard correctly.

"Of course, I did," Mark circled his hand. His annoyance raised a notch. The woman proved a bit dense in some matters.

"It isn't like you weren't through a nightmare last night, Ella. You need to recover, and besides, I'm sorry to tell you this, but that side of your face is badly swollen and bruised. I didn't think you'd want everybody to see you like this," he explained.

Ella blinked, trying to find her voice. She didn't know what to say, though. The young woman wanted to shout at him. She felt like hitting him and throwing something. However, she was also wearied, not only in a bad mood.

"Mark," she started slowly. "You can't make decisions on my behalf. If I can't go to work, I will call in sick, not you." By now, she started raising her voice, and Mark's brows rose on his forehead. "Who, the hell, do you think you are to call my boss and tell him that I'm sick?"

"Okay, calm down," Mark said, putting his hands up. "I might have stepped over the line, but you had a fretful sleep all night. Only in the morning, you calmed down," he explained to her.

He stroked her arms to soothe her and thought of kissing the corner of her mouth but changed his mind. The woman didn't seem amiable to that.

"I thought I shouldn't wake you and ask to decide what you wanted to do. You needn't go over the bend like that," Mark continued in a steely voice. "If you want me to go, I'll go. It isn't such a big deal. You don't have to make a dramatic scene out of this."

Ella didn't like where things were going and panicked. She didn't know if she overreacted, but she knew that Mark had helped her, over and over again.

She rubbed her face and then told him, "I don't know what to say, Mark. I really don't. I know that I need a shower and a cup of coffee. Maybe I'll get my wits back then, and I'll know what I want to tell you."

He stared at her with the same steely eyes for a few more seconds and then nodded. His tense muscles relaxed, and he stroked her hair.

"Go, have your shower, and I'll make the coffee," he finally said and turned away.

Ella's gaze followed him until he left the bedroom, and then, she leaned on the bathroom door and closed her eyes. She had a piercing pain in her temples and behind her eyes, and her swollen cheek was throbbing. The headache was back.

She was confused and upset. She didn't know what to do anymore, and suddenly, everything seemed too much. Tears pooled in her eyes. When the first tear ran down her face, she closed the bathroom door and turned on the shower tap.

CHAPTER TWELVE

ELLA CAME INTO THE living room, and Mark's eyes assessed her from the top of her head to the tip of her toes. She wasn't used to such scrutiny and started fidgeting. Satisfied, Mark nodded, grabbing another cup to pour coffee for Ella. Then he piled the cups, a sugar bowl, and a milk jug on a tray. Tilting his head, he invited her out on the balcony.

"Let's go outside, Ella. It's warm enough for the beginning of October," he observed. "I'm pretty sure that you can use some fresh air."

Ella didn't reply but followed him outside, where she sat in one of the lawn armchairs on the balcony. The woman put sugar and milk in the coffee he put in front of her. She breathed the smell of the lake deeply, welcoming the smooth breeze on her skin.

"Still upset with me?" Mark inquired. His tone warned her that, either way, it was all right with him. He didn't care.

She shook her head. She wasn't upset with him anymore. She had been angry before, but she had chosen to believe that he had done what he did for her own good. She could swallow his actions better that way.

Anyway, she would have probably requested the day off. Nevertheless, she needed to make sure that he understood that he couldn't make decisions in her place.

"I'm not upset anymore, Mark," Ella shook her head, gazing directly into his eyes. "However," she stressed out the word, "please, don't make any more decisions for me. Just ask me first."

Mark studied her for a few seconds, and then, he acknowledged her wishes with a nod.

"All right, no more decisions without asking you first. Got it! Now, what are you saying if we have a light breakfast? That's the code for some toast and butter. That's the sum of my efforts in the kitchen for breakfast. Then we could go out for a walk along the lake and have a late lunch somewhere. What are you saying?" he asked her, taking her left hand in his and playing with her fingers.

Despite her constant headache, her skin tingled at the feel of his fingers on her skin. She couldn't make sense of the effect that Mark had on her. That was another thing she didn't understand.

Ella knew that she hadn't felt half of that desire for Colin, even during the best days of their relationship. She had been with Colin for far more time, and she knew that feelings needed time to evolve.

Sometimes, she had the impression that Mark felt the same way, but doubts overwhelmed her other times. He behaved like he didn't feel anything at all for her. He was just a player trying to score and move on.

That constant roller-coaster of feelings was driving her crazy. She loathed the endless guessing and the doubts rolling in her mind all the time.

Ella got so lost in her thoughts that Mark waved his hand in front of her eyes.

"Hey, are you still here with me? Where have you gone, Ella?"

She laughed, but her laughter sounded somehow strained in her ears, and she didn't doubt that he felt that too.

"Yes, I am here. Of course, I am here. Let's go, yeah. I'll have to change my clothes first, but it's a good idea. Let's go out. Maybe a stroll will help with my headache," Ella stood up, determined to push her thoughts away. She would take Mark the way he was, at least for that day.

"Still painful?" he inquired. "You'd better take two more Tylenol."

"Yep, daddy, I will," she joked, but her words didn't bring a smile to his lips, so she rushed inside to change her clothes.

Ella didn't bother to wonder about what he was thinking right then. She would probably find out soon enough.

THEY STROLLED ON THE waterfront for about half an hour, and Ella felt grateful that Mark had made her take her jacket. The wind had picked up, and the air was chilly.

They talked a lot, and Mark made up stories about the people around, making her laugh. The man had a good imagination and made good use of it. His stories were full of humour and made her feel better.

"You should have been a writer," Ella remarked. "You have a knack for bringing stories alive."

"Maybe I was a writer in another life," he said with a grin and shrugged.

"You believe in reincarnation," she noted nonplussed, unable to hide her surprise at his words.

"I can't say I do, but I can't say I don't, either," Mark replied, and then, he steered her towards the Irish Pub open near the quay.

"What does that mean?" Ella asked, laughing with skepticism. "You don't make any sense. You believe something, or you don't. There's nothing in between."

"But I do make sense if you think a little," Mark countered, always grinning at her. "I can't say that I believe because I haven't experienced it firsthand. Therefore, I don't have solid proof. However, I can't say that I don't because I don't have definite proof that reincarnation isn't possible."

"That's... a bit farfetched, Mark," Ella said. "Considering your theory, you can say the same thing for a lot of things."

"Yep, and I do," he confirmed. "Ghosts, a greater power, a living universe, extraterrestrial life... and it goes on and on. I have an extensive list," he declared with a chuckle.

"You're just making fun of me," Ella replied, and she narrowed her eyes to slits.

"Far from it," he told her and stopped walking. He took both her hands in his and gazed into her eyes with seriousness. "Ella, I think that there are lots of things out there, and no one can explain or prove them," he explained.

Mark brushed the tips of his fingers over the back of her hand for a few seconds, pensively. Then, he looked over to the grey surface of the lake for a few seconds, lost in thought.

Ella couldn't think of an answer, so she just watched him with curiosity. That was a facet he had never shown to her.

"However," his eyes turned to her, "I can't deny any of those things just because I can't see them. I prefer to..." he shook his head, trying to find his words. "How can I say it so you'd understand what I mean?" he said, shifting his eyes to a point in the distance. "Look, I don't write anything off just because someone says that a thing is not possible. Remember Shakespeare."

Ella looked at him, dumbfounded, "Shakespeare?"

"Yes, Shakespeare. 'There are more things in heaven and earth, Horatio/Than are dreamt of in your philosophy.' Hamlet said that to Horatio."

"Yes, of course, I know that, but I don't see the connection."

"It's like this, Ella. To disapprove of something, I need incontestable proof. I won't do it because someone says so.

I prefer circumspection," Mark said.

He thought a couple of minutes, and then he continued.

"I'm sure there's much more in this world or beyond this world than what I can ever imagine," he shook his head. "Just think about it. All the time, progress in science shows that something previously considered a hoax, it is an actual fact," Mark pointed out.

The man's fingers brushed Ella's while he gathered his thoughts.

"They were damn sure that the Earth was flat. It turned out it was round or approximately round. Then, they considered that the Sun circled the Earth, and Earth was the center of the universe. Well, science showed differently. These are the most common examples. So, no, I can't say I believe, or I don't believe in something just because people declare that something is impossible. I need to see proof. I'm a Doubting Thomas in absolutely everything."

Ella gazed at him pensively. Suddenly, she saw something more in him, although somewhat disturbing. She understood that he wouldn't take anything at face value without necessary proof, and that would be valid, especially for feelings.

"What?" he asked when he noticed how her eyes scrutinized him.

She shrugged and shook the sad thoughts out of her mind. With a smile, she replied, "Nothing, you've revealed something new about yourself, and it's thrilling and scary at the same time," she admitted.

"Thrilling and scary," he repeated musingly. "That's interesting. Why?"

She started walking, and he followed her.

"I don't know how to explain it, Mark, but... It's like I've just seen that there is a new dimension to you...," she replied without looking at him.

Ella didn't even see where she was going. Her thoughts were in turmoil, and she felt an unusual pressure in her chest.

"Deeper, if you want. Nevertheless, what you've said explains your difficulty connecting to someone and building a serious relationship. That worries me," the young woman confessed. Ella glanced at Mark and saw him frown.

"Might be," he said. "But there's always more than it meets the eye to everyone. I might have more reasons than you think for my difficulty to connect to someone," he continued. "Anyway, let's have a late lunch and talk some more," Mark pulled her into the pub.

The hostess showed them to a table while Ella fought with herself, not sure whether she should ask more questions or not. She lost.

"Okay, you made me curious. What other reasons?"

Mark glanced at her. He picked up the menu the hostess left on the table and opened it.

"I don't want to be rude, Ella, but that's personal," he said, and his curt voice chilled her to the bones.

Ella grabbed her menu off the table, as well. She opened it and tried to read it. However, she didn't see anything before her eyes.

Suddenly, she wanted to leave and go home alone. Now, she had definitive evidence that the relationship she believed she had built with Mark was just an illusion.

Ella was very deep in her thoughts, and when he touched her hand, she winced. With a gasp, she turned her wide eyes to him.

"I'm sorry, Ella. I didn't mean to upset you. That's something I don't talk about," Mark said to her. "It doesn't have anything to do with you. Believe me. It's just something from the past, and it's a past I'm trying to forget," he explained, and sincerity rang in his voice.

Ella shifted her eyes back at her menu and said in a very matter-of-fact tone of voice, "I think I feel like a steak, Mark. I know they have the best New York steak here."

"Ella," Mark insisted, but she pulled her hand from his and looked directly into his eyes.

"It isn't a problem, Mark. All of us have secrets and aren't willing to share them with unimportant people," she replied in a clipped tone of voice.

"I've never said that you were unimportant," he replied with exasperation. "I've just said that the subject wasn't important."

"No, you didn't, and it isn't," she replied very matter-of-factly. "Don't worry, Mark, you can keep your secrets. Let's eat something. I'm famished."

Mark wanted to insist and make her understand but realized that it wouldn't do any good to him. He signalled to the waitress to come and take their order.

"What would you like to drink?" he asked Ella.

"Some Coke would be nice, I think," she replied.

"Two Cokes, please," he ordered, and with a nod, the waitress scribbled something on her pad and left to give their orders to the kitchen.

Ella looked everywhere but in his direction. Mark grabbed her hand, and despite her efforts to pull it back, he held on to it fast.

"All right, Ella," he said, and uncertainty rang in his voice. "I haven't told this to anyone else before, not even to my closest friends," he pointed out and then hesitated for a few seconds.

His eyes swept over the people in the restaurant and then came back to her.

"Some time back, I was about to get married...."

Ella practically flinched at his words. They shocked her. Ella expected something on the lines of a broken love affair, but nothing so big.

"Don't tell me that she left you at the altar or anything like that," she asked him, afraid of what he would reveal. Ella knew that some wounds needed a very long time to heal, and some never healed completely.

Mark chuckled bitterly. "No, nothing like that," he replied. "Two weeks before the marriage, I decided to have lunch in a Chinese restaurant. Just a hankering, you know. There wasn't any near my office, so I took a taxi to the Mandarin. You know, that one where you can eat as much as you want, and it costs almost nothing. Anyway, good food, I must say. I'm crazy about it, although I always regret overeating when I leave the restaurant. Anyways, I got there and got in line, waiting to be seated, you know, when I heard the voice of my sweet fiancé," he said.

Ella's ears pricked. The sarcasm in Mark's voice worried her, and the thin hairs at the back of her neck stood up.

"She was there, you see," he said. "She was talking to one of her close friends, explaining to her that she couldn't wait to get married to me," Mark said and shook his head.

He chuckled, but his laughter didn't sound happy at all, and her heart cringed. He shook his head once more, and then, he continued.

"Imagine that my heart soared at that moment. It felt good to hear the woman you wanted to marry say something like that. My heart soared, only to fall, very, very down, just a few moments afterwards," his brows bunched over his eyes. His glance turned to the people in the restaurant for a few seconds.

Ella understood that Mark needed time before going on with the story, and that told her that what she was about to hear wouldn't be easy to swallow.

Mark's eyes turned back at her. His mouth was a thin line, and a muscle twitched in his jaw.

"Well, she went on and explained everything to her friend. She had a plan, you see," he shrugged as if didn't matter.

Nonetheless, Ella knew that it mattered. That woman's words had scarred the man for life.

"She planned to marry me, indeed," he nodded, and Ella's eyes widened.

That wasn't what she expected. She shook herself mentally. She decided not to make assumptions anymore but waited for Mark to tell the story.

"Yep, she wanted to marry me and make my life a living hell. Once she achieved that purpose, she would have divorced me and taken me for everything I had," he said bitterly with another shake of his head. "There was no prenup in place, so I'd have paid and paid, probably for my entire life," he admitted with disdain for himself.

Ella shook her head, unable to process everything so fast. She knew that people like that existed. However, she had never met one in her personal life, and she needed time to reflect upon that situation's facets.

Mark tossed his head and said, "I was just a meal ticket for her, you understand. So, I broke that so-called relationship, right there, that very moment. I cancelled the wedding and went on my merry way. So, that's everything, nothing more."

Ella just kept looking at him, and that made Mark uncomfortable. If she had said something at least, he would have known what she thought, but her silence was ominous.

"Did you love her a lot? Do you still love her?" she asked after a few more minutes of silence.

Her words stunned him, and he stared at her, unable to reply immediately. He had expected something else from her, anything else but that.

He gathered his wits and asked, "What?"

"You still love her, don't you?" Ella stated with sadness and resignation in her voice.

"Are you out of your mind?" Mark asked, practically shouting.

Her assumption astounded him. He raised his brows, and disbelief shone in his eyes.

"How, the heck, have you got to that conclusion? Even if I loved her before, I wouldn't have after discovering what she had planned. But it turned out that I never loved her," Mark said with a sarcastic sneer. "I was just flattered that she looked at me. You know the type, something like your friend, Jo, if I remember her name correctly," he said with a grin.

Ella felt that Mark was telling the truth. Still, he didn't know Jo.

"You're wrong, Mark. Jo wouldn't do something like that. She's snooty, but she doesn't use people. If she likes someone, she's honest. She's never been in love, but she'd be loyal and protective if she were."

Mark tilted his head as if he accepted the reprimand, and his attitude wasn't far from the truth. His contact with Jo had been marginal. So he couldn't judge the woman after a few minutes of conversation, even though that conversation had revealed a very narrow-minded person, in his opinion.

Then, he retook her hand. He gazed straight into her eyes and said, "I'm not heartbroken, Ella. I merely don't think this is the right time for me to have a steady relationship. I am not looking to get married, you know. However, I'd love for us to move on to the next stage of our relationship. We know each other well enough now, don't you think?"

Ella looked at him and said nothing. She didn't even know what to answer. For the first time in her life, a man was telling her that he thought their relationship should evolve, and at the same time, he admitted that he didn't want to go steady. If that wasn't a contradiction in terms, she didn't know what it was.

"Ella," Mark tried to make her answer to him by pulling her hand.

She turned her eyes on him and replied in a calm tone of voice, "So, what you want is a sort of relationship, something with benefits from what I understand. What you do is warn me that I shouldn't think of happily ever after. Correct?"

"I didn't formulate it like that, though," he smiled at her. Nevertheless, his smile wasn't so sincere this time. "Yet, we know each other well enough by now. People live together for a lifetime and don't know everything about each other. And we like each other. You can't deny it," he pushed some more. His unnerving gaze held hers with determination.

"There's chemistry between us, Ella," Mark pointed out. "And to be honest, it's a strong chemistry," he continued persuasively.

His words were valid at some level. Ella didn't say anything but merely looked at him. She didn't even know what to say. Still, she did want a little more from a relationship.

"Come on, Ella. Let's make a final check here," Mark said.

To her amazement, Mark started counting the reasons on his fingers.

"We are good together most of the time. We laugh together; we talk about things; we don't get bored with each other, and we are attracted to each other," the man said, checking everything on one finger at a time. "So, I'd say that we should give it a try," he pleaded. "I could lie to you and say that I want forever," he shrugged. "Would that make you feel better?" he asked her with sarcasm in his voice.

"No, Mark, lying wouldn't make me feel better, of course," she replied, matching his matter-of-fact tone of voice. "Nonetheless, knowing that there might be a possibility for more, not now, I understand that," she hurried to say. "But later on, yes, that would make me feel better."

"That would be lying," he persisted with a frown between his brows. "No one can know what later will bring, Ella. What we have, it's now. That's all we have. And now, it's good," he said, gesticulating between the two of them.

His words didn't change her mind, and he could see it. However, he believed that he still might have a chance to convince her.

"Come on! We get along well enough. Why not explore it more?" Mark opened his arms.

"Look," Ella replied, a little upset now. "I'm not a prude. And yes, I'm attracted to you. Nevertheless, I don't like that you are closing the door to something before it's time to close it."

"But I'm not," he answered. "What I'm doing is to tell what I think and feel. This is me, and what you see now, it's what you can be sure about me. The rest ... you never know what might be."

Ella wanted to reply but noticed the waitress bringing their orders, so she leaned back in her chair and kept quiet.

Mark read in her eyes what was going on. He turned his head just in time to see the waitress near his chair. He smiled at her and made room to put the food on the table.

"Will this be all?" she asked.

Satisfied, Ella noticed that the woman looked at her first and then Mark. At least, she had some manners, and Ella liked her for that, so she smiled warmly at her.

"I'm fine, thank you," she answered, and Mark nodded his agreement.

They started eating in silence, but it didn't last long. There was always something to be said or discussed. Ella and Mark always found something that made them laugh together.

Ella had to admit that Mark was right. They had something good going between them, and no one knew what would happen in the end.

She had taken a risk before when she thought everything would be great. She had been wrong.

Despite that, she had to take a risk with Mark now. She had never responded so strongly to another man. It would have been a pity to break up with him because he couldn't commit to something more.

Ella didn't want to live with regrets. She knew she would if she gave up the relationship with Mark before anything terrible happened. She would always wonder about what could have been.

"SO, WHAT WOULD YOU like to do now?" Mark asked after they left the pub. "Do you want to go back home, or would you like to walk a little more?"

Ella thought for a few moments and then said, "No, let's go home. If that's all right with you, of course," she added.

"Yep, it is," he answered with a grin and took her hand. "We can have a coffee on your balcony. If you're not tired, we could watch a movie later. What do you think?"

"All right, coffee and movie are fine," she agreed with his idea.

The wind had picked up some more, and the breeze made her shiver. Mark felt she was trembling, and letting go of her hand, he slid his arm around her shoulders and gathered her to him.

"It's getting colder every day," he remarked. "This weather is very treacherous. You think it would be warm, and suddenly, you freeze, especially here on the shore of the lake. It's the wind, I think."

Ella nodded and snuggled into him. Mark made her feel protected and warm, a feeling she hadn't had for a long time.

They got inside her condo, and after they closed the door, Mark stopped her and took her face in his hands. He looked into her eyes for a few long seconds, and then, he leaned and kissed her lips. It was a feather-like kiss, barely there, but her nerves started to hum.

Ella slipped her hands upward to his shoulders. On tiptoes, she shut her eyes and returned his kiss. His mouth became bolder and greedy, and he deepened his kiss.

His musky smell blended with the scent left by the wind in his hair and filled Ella's nostrils. His fingers stroked her exposed skin slowly, and all her senses went in overdrive.

Ella had been kissed before, and she liked kissing. She had always believed that a kiss was more intimate than anything. Yet, she had never felt so strung and so filled with expectation as she felt right then.

Mark changed the angle of his mouth on hers, and his teeth bit just a bit sharper into her lower lip. She moaned, and in response, Mark shaped his body to hers. She shivered, feeling the hard planes of his chest and the pressure of his lower body.

Mark leaned his head to her so that his forehead touched Ella's. He tasted her and nibbled at her lips with an insatiable hunger. Then he pulled a hair away from her mouth, breathing hard.

They remained like that, tightly holding each other for a few long minutes. Only their difficult breathing pierced the silence that stretched around them, swirling in the room.

After a while, Mark pulled back at arm's length and grinned at her mischievously. Suddenly, he picked her up in his arms, surprising her, and Ella yelped. She knotted her arms behind his neck, afraid that he would drop her, and he burst into laughter.

"Don't be afraid, Ella! You're too tiny for me to drop."

Ella merely shook her head, and Mark strode to the bedroom with her in his arms. He held her close to his chest, his gaze trained on her face. However, the man stopped before going through the door. "Are we on the same page here, Ella?" he asked her in a grave tone of voice. "You know that I want you badly, but if you don't want me...."

"I do," she answered hastily, afraid that he would change his mind. He let out an exaggerated relieved sigh, and she laughed.

Mark carried her inside the bedroom and let her stand near the bed. He looked at her with so much intensity that she got warmer under his gaze. With the tip of a finger, the man touched the left side of her face carefully, as if he were afraid that he would hurt her. After a few moments, he brushed her hair back.

Always gazing into her eyes, Mark got closer, and his lips brushed her cheek and then her ear. He ended with a bite of her earlobe, and Ella trembled once more.

Mark's fingers massaged the back of her head, and his lips descended along her neck with feather-like touches. His teeth sank into the sensitive skin, and Ella moaned. Mark licked the abused skin, and Ella stopped thinking.

ELLA AND MARK SAW EACH other almost every day in the following weeks. Mark would invite her out for dinner, or sometimes, to a movie, or just a stroll. Other times, they would make dinner together.

Mark would spend almost every night with her. They would laugh, sharing the events that happened during the day. Ella didn't see any sign that he had had enough and intended to move on.

They were good together, and Ella believed they were meant for each other. She would surprise herself daydreaming of a future with Mark and needed to get back with her feet on the ground.

Ella hoped to share her life with him, not only because of her biological clock, which kept ticking. But for the first time in her life, she felt good with a man in and out of bed.

Yet, Mark never hinted at a future together, and Ella didn't want to broach the subject, afraid that she would jinx what they already had.

After all, Mark had been clear from the beginning, and he hadn't given her any false hopes. He hadn't tried to lie and make her believe that having a life together in the years to come would be an option.

Ella felt satisfied, although she hadn't fulfilled her expectations entirely. Nevertheless, something bothered her, and that obsession marred somewhat the moments she shared with him. Mark never invited her to his house. She didn't even know exactly where he worked or what he did for a living. He hinted at some things or others, but he was never clear about anything.

However, days turned into weeks, and a month stretched into two. December came, and they were still together, their relationship growing stronger by the day.

Whenever she looked in the mirror, Ella noticed that she was glowing. She looked better than ever before, and she knew that Mark had put that glow on her face. She also knew that she was hopelessly in love with him.

CHAPTER THIRTEEN

ELLA HURRIED INTO THE conference room, trying to catch her breath. She was late, although she had been running to get there. That hadn't happened in her entire career. She might have been late a few minutes when she met her friends, but not for business meetings.

Everything had gone wrong that morning. Ella didn't need the alarm to wake up, but she didn't even hear it that day.

She woke up an hour and fifteen minutes late, so she rushed through her morning routine to gain time.

Mark hadn't spent the night before with her because he had to meet one of his good friends. Otherwise, at least, he would have woken her up.

Ella used to take the shuttle to the subway in the morning, but the shuttle had already left when she got downstairs, so she hurried to the streetcar as she didn't want to take her car out. She knew she would have spent most of the time stuck in traffic, and that wouldn't have helped at all.

She was out of luck, though. The streetcar also got stuck in traffic because of an accident on the rail. So she had to walk to the subway. That took her over twenty minutes.

Walking in heels for so long wasn't easy, and Ella cursed herself for not wearing comfortable boots. It had snowed over the night. The snow had already melted, but the pavement was slippery.

Ella had to go and meet her boss at a rival firm where they had a meeting for a divorce settlement. She knocked just in passing on the conference room door the receptionist had shown to her and opened the door at the same time.

Ella strode inside the room but stopped in shock before reaching the table. She had already opened her mouth to apologize, but no word came off her numb lips. Wide-eyed, Ella stared at Mark. He sat at the table next to the other party in the divorce case.

Mark's eyes didn't show any recollection. He merely assessed her coldly. They had met not earlier than two days before, and now, he reacted to her presence as if she were a mere employee. She didn't deserve more than a superficial perusal.

Ella stumbled but recovered immediately and finally managed to speak. "I apologize for being late. The traffic was awful. I hope you haven't waited for too long."

"Don't worry, Ella. We've been here for just a few minutes," her boss replied in a jovial tone of voice. "Have a seat, and as soon as the receptionist brings the coffee in, we will start," he waved her to the seat next to their client, Mrs. Thompson.

Their client, a fifty-five-year-old woman, had long ago left her youth behind. The lines on her face revealed an uncomfortable and challenging life.

MR. RIGHT

Mrs. Thompson had reached out to the Pro Bono Ontario organization. She pleaded for help when her husband started the divorce procedures after over twenty-eight years of marriage, during which she had supported him in any way she could.

She had worked double shifts in a bar for over three years while he attended university. Then she had raised four children, keeping an immaculate house for her family. The woman had also helped him move up into his world, organizing the perfect parties he desired and demanded.

Well, after almost three decades of faithful marriage and dedication from her side, her husband found the perfect way to show his gratitude to his wife. Mr. Thompson went through a middle-age crisis and started dating young women. Consequently, he found the woman of his dreams, and he couldn't live without her.

The man asked for a divorce immediately. During the procedures, he made it clear that his wife, for nearly thirty years, didn't deserve much in exchange for her hard work.

The man had made her life a living hell for over a year until she moved out. He waited just for that to crush her methodically. Throwing her into the street and turning her into a beggar became his life mission.

The man closed the joint accounts and left her penniless. And now, all her hard work was about to be rewarded with a last fatal blow.

However, someone introduced Mrs. Thompson to Ella's boss, who volunteered pro bono in such situations. He wasn't a facile opponent.

Ella believed that Mr. Lloyd would preserve some of the family's financial assets and help the ex-wife obtain shelter and have food on the table, at least.

However, she didn't know what Mark was doing there in the conference room and his position in the proceedings.

The coffee came, and the negotiations began. Their client's bitterness and the opponent's sarcasm stalled the discussions.

Mark spoke in the husband's favour, explaining that he was on the man's side and would make his case if necessary.

In the end, Mr. Lloyd determined that they couldn't reach an agreement and would have to go to court.

The meeting exhausted Ella. Raw emotions flew wildly, and the constant dish on the menu consisted of recriminations and insults.

During the discussions, Ella found out that Mark was a reputable software company owner. It had been the talk of the town for the last couple of years. Even Ella had heard about it.

The man's vision had built some popular apps and created software for critical industries. Besides, his company developed games and hogged a large slice of that market.

Ella had thought that she knew who Mark was. She had believed that he was a well-paid guy, employed in a good position in a big company, even though he had never said anything.

Yet, she had noticed his high-quality clothes and his choice of venues when they went out together. He would choose from the cheapest but tastiest fast-food restaurants to the most elegant ones.

The reality went beyond Ella's wildest theories. It also hurt her that Mark had decided to keep her in the dark.

Yes, she could understand why he had done it. He had been seriously hurt in the past and didn't trust any woman now.

Nevertheless, she resented his attitude, and she resented him. Mark should have known her already. Ella wasn't a materialistic woman. She had never asked for anything and preferred to rely on herself.

Ella couldn't wait to step out of that conference room. She couldn't breathe but wanted to confront Mark and dish everything out. Her pain was close to the surface, and she might say things that she would regret after a while. So, she didn't know if that was a good idea.

She left the room with Mr. Lloyd and their client. In the elevator, in a soft tone of voice, Mr. Lloyd explained to Mrs. Thompson what would happen next. He told her that things might have looked bad, but they weren't.

The poor woman was worried and scared witless, so Mr. Lloyd invited her to his office to continue their discussion and ease her mind.

When they exited the elevator, he turned to Ella. "I'll take Mrs. Thompson to the office in my car, Ella. I don't think you have anything urgent to do today. Anyway, you've done a great job lately, so I'm going to give you the day off. So, go home and relax. Tomorrow, you'll have enough work to do. You deserve a break. Do you need a ride somewhere?"

Ella thanked him but declined his offer. She went out of the building, and the other two took another elevator to the parking lot.

Ella stopped in front of the building, unsure of what to do with her time that day. She was happy she didn't have to go to work. Her thoughts wandered other trails. However, she was also afraid that her mind would churn over questions and doubts with so much free time on her hands.

A hand landed on her shoulder, and startled, she turned and met Mark's deep eyes. She shook his hand off and narrowed her eyes to slits.

"You didn't seem to remember me when I came into that room, so what do you want with me now?"

"Come on, Ella. That was just business. I'm sure you can understand that," Mark replied, a small smile in the corner of his mouth.

Ella gazed back at him with cold eyes and replied, "Yeah, everything is just business. Well, I think you've just struck out, Mark. I'm closed for business right now."

She turned her back to him and went down the stairs carefully so that she wouldn't slip and fall. The steps had been cleaned of snow, but they were still slippery.

Mark came after her and grasped her arm. "All right, why are you upset now? Help me understand. Is it because I didn't say something like 'Hi, Ella, did you have a good night? And what do you think about drinks after?' Is that what this is about?" he asked with a hard glint in his eyes.

"Let go of me, Mark," she shook off his arm again. "No, I didn't expect you to say that. But then, I didn't expect you to react as if I were just a pesky employee beneath your station." Ella cringed inwardly, listening to her own cantankerous tone.

Ella didn't want to let him know how much he had annoyed and hurt her. It was as if she praised him for a job well done.

"I didn't react like that, and you know it. There's something else gnawing at you, isn't there?" Mark replied with a scowl.

Ella considered the wisdom of revealing what she felt and decided to go with the truth. She had asked him to be honest with her, so she had to be frank herself.

"All right, Mark. The problem is that you lied to me. You never said who you were. Was it because you were afraid I'd turn into your ex-fiancée or what?" she ended her tirade.

"I have never lied, Ella, and you know it. I've just never come out to say that I was that or another," he pointed out.

"You omitted some details, Mark, yes. But that's also lying."

"Not from where I'm standing, no," he replied unruffled.

"Great, then we agree to disagree. Now, I have some things to do, so ... goodbye," Ella said and turned her back to him, looking for a taxi. She didn't feel like making the trip back home by public transport.

"Will we talk later?" Mark asked from behind her.

She turned her head to him, looked at him pensively for a few seconds, and then she said, "No, we won't."

She turned her attention to the street and finally spied a taxi. She stopped it and got inside the car without looking back at Mark.

CHAPTER FOURTEEN

MARK WAITED FOR A COUPLE of days to give Ella the time to cool down. He hoped he would have a better chance to speak to her now. He thought that the wound wouldn't be so fresh, and the woman might listen to him for a change.

For the last couple of days, Mark had been thinking about what happened the last time they saw each other. He had to admit that he would have been furious as hell if he had been in her shoes. He knew that he had only one chance to get things right and get back to the status quo they shared before.

Now Mark paced in front of her building, waiting for someone to come and go inside so that he could take advantage and go through the open door. He had already concocted a sappy story about a surprise and an anniversary. He didn't doubt that he would sway the concierge to allow him to go upstairs without announcing him first.

Mark had come with flowers, and not only to support his story. On the day he quarrelled with Ella, he sent her a bouquet of white roses. He hoped that she would get the message behind the flowers. Mark wanted to apologize. He understood that he was guilty of what had happened.

The day before, he sent another bouquet, and this time he made it of yellow roses. He didn't exactly know why yellow, but that was how he felt.

Mark didn't have any practice in apologizing or grovelling. He could charm the panties off any woman, but he never apologized for anything. Now, he brought red roses, hoping that they would plead his case with more success than his words.

The man strolled in front of the building until he spied a woman with two children going into the lobby. He sighed with relief and followed them immediately.

The concierge glanced in their direction, but he didn't try to stop Mark. He merely greeted the woman and nodded to Mark, smiling.

Mark thanked the heavens for his luck. He thought that maybe the man had seen him come into the building often and assumed that Ella approved of his going upstairs to her apartment. Apparently, Ella hadn't announced to the concierge that Mark was persona non grata now.

Mark's luck seemed to hold fast. The woman and the children started toward the south tower, so Mark got to the elevators without asking for the concierge's permission.

Mark sighed with relief when the woman and her brood got out of the elevator on the fifth floor. They had been so nosy that Mark couldn't gather his thoughts.

He had gritted his teeth all the time. He needed his wits about him to convince Ella to take him back into her life.

Mark wasn't ready to let Ella go. He had realized that sorry fact in less than a couple of hours after their last discussion.

Mark's patience was wearing thin, and when the elevator finally stopped at Ella's floor, he strode with determination along the corridor toward the door of her apartment. He breathed deeply and raised his hand to knock, only to have the door thrown open suddenly in front of him and hear Ella shout from the top of her lungs.

"I've told you never to come back here, Colin. I've told you we were through. I don't know what was in that concierge's mind to let you come upstairs, but I'll take care of him too, don't worry."

"Come on, baby," Colin replied, with a smile in his voice. "You know you missed me and want me back. I bumped into your mom a couple of days ago, and she told me everything about that. You don't have to play coy with me now."

"You're out of your mind if you took her word over mine. You should have known by now that I don't confide in her about anything."

Mark listened, mesmerized. Ella and the unknown guy were engrossed in their discussion, and they didn't even notice that they had an audience.

Mark cleared his throat to attract their attention. Ella turned her head sharply, and a sudden blush painted her cheeks. Embarrassment made her swallow hard.

She hated that Mark had witnessed her outburst. She had hoped that her banshee-like days would finish after throwing Colin out of her house.

Colin came near her and glanced at Mark first and then at the bouquet of roses in his hand.

"Who the hell is this, Ella? Are you cheating on me?" he barked, turning his thunderous eyes back to her.

Ella's eyes widened with shock, and a weight lifted off Mark's heart. For a moment there, he thought that Ella had made a fool out of him. After the episode with Gina, he had promised himself not to let that ever happen to him again.

"What?" Ella recovered her voice and shouted at the man. "Have you completely lost your senses, Colin? Do I have to break something over your head to make you come back to reality? You ... you, stupid! How the heck I'm cheating on you when we broke up months ago?" she snapped back at him.

"We didn't, Ella," Colin countered in a harsh tone of voice, scowling at her. "I've just given you some time to get back to your senses, that's all."

"You're out of your mind," she shook her head in disbelief. "I've had my doubts before, but now I know for sure. I threw you out of my house, you idiot, and I meant it," she pointed her finger to the door to show him out again.

Ella would throw Colin out of her house to make the cretin understand. She didn't want to get violent with him, but she did what she had to.

"Get it through your puny brain, Colin. We're through, so never come back or talk to me again. I'll take a restraining order against you if necessary," she told him, shaking with pent-up fury.

Colin's eyes narrowed dangerously. Without warning, the man backhanded Ella hard. She fell, and her head hit the wall with a thump. She yelped, and not only because of the pain. She hadn't expected the man to react violently, and Colin's behaviour stunned her.

Mark practically growled and advanced toward them. He didn't look at Ella but kept his eyes trained on Colin. Without ceremony, he thrust the flowers to Ella. Swiftly, the fingers of his right hand curled tightly around Colin's neck, and Ella's eyes bulged in shock. She couldn't believe what was happening, and her legs shook like spaghetti.

Mark shoved Colin into the wall opposite Ella. Always holding his fingers tight around the man's throat, he lifted the man an inch above the floor. His actions seemed effortless, and Ella could do nothing but stare.

Colin was so scared that his eyes nearly popped out of their sockets. The man's belligerence had vanished, and he shook visibly. Colin became aware that he couldn't fight against Mark.

He pissed his pants, and a pungent smell filled the air. Mark scowled, and his lips curled with disgust. He pushed Colin out of the door. The man splashed into a heap in the middle of the corridor.

"Stay away from her, punk," Mark said in a steely voice. "If I hear that you dared to look at her, it will be my pleasure to rip your limbs off one by one. Do you hear me?" he asked in a roar.

Colin scrambled to gain his feet. He stood and nodded like a puppet on strings, and then he ran to the elevator. He just wanted to get away from Mark.

Tears filled his eyes, vindictive thoughts ran through his mind, and his helplessness brought fresh sweat to his forehead. Nevertheless, Colin knew that he was essentially a coward at heart. He wouldn't do anything about it. The man clenched his teeth, and his hands fisted.

Mark's narrowed eyes followed Colin's progress along the corridor and then turned to Ella. She hadn't moved from where he had left her. She was still holding the flowers as if they were her lifeline.

Ella stared at Mark, her eyes wide and her mouth agape. The print of Colin's palm still coloured the side of her face, and Mark touched the spot tenderly. He didn't want to hurt her unnecessarily.

"Are you all right, Ella?" the man asked softly.

She nodded, although she didn't feel all right at all. Colin's behaviour and words had shocked her, and Mark's unexpected reaction had stolen her voice.

Ella didn't know whether she should be grateful that Mark had appeared at her door. However, she couldn't deny that she was beyond thankful that Colin was out of her life again, and probably, for good that time.

She didn't know what her mother saw in Colin, but she seemed to be the only one who liked and cheered for the prick. No one else in Ella's family or of her friends could stand the sight of him, and some of them had been rather vocal against him.

Her mother's interference in her life annoyed and angered Ella. It wasn't for the first time, and Ella doubted that it would be for the last time. Nevertheless, she knew that talking to her mother about that wouldn't do any good.

"Ella, are you okay, baby?" Mark's voice finally reached her. She shook off her thoughts and looked up at him.

"Yes, I'm fine, Mark. Thank you for throwing that piece of garbage out of the door," she said and tilted her head. Then she pursed her lips and wiped off her damp forehead.

Ella remembered that she was still holding the flowers Mark had nearly thrown at her and shook her head. She strode with long steps to the kitchen to put the roses in water, and Mark followed her.

"I suppose you brought the flowers for me," she said with impatience, turning to him before shoving the roses into a vase.

"Of course, they're for you," Mark smiled at her. "I certainly didn't bring them for Colin," he made a shabby attempt to humour, and she rewarded him with a weak smile. "Come on, Ella, are you sure you're okay?" he came to her, laying a hand on her arm. "The idiot threw you pretty hard into the wall," Mark added with worry in his voice, and the tips of his fingers brushed the side of her face once more.

"Not much harm done," Ella tried to lighten up his mood, waving his concerns away.

Then, she took a vase off a shelf and arranged the flowers in the vase. An uncertain smile lingered on her curved lips and drove Mark crazy. He couldn't judge her mood at all.

"Luckily, I have more than one vase, Mark," she shook her head. "I wouldn't have known what to do with all the flowers you sent me otherwise," she turned her smile to him after she finished with the roses.

Ella looked around for an available surface to display the flowers. Then she put the vase stuffed with roses on the kitchen counter.

Mark grinned mischievously at her. "Well, I did get into a big blunder the other day, so... I had to apologize, and big time," he admitted.

"You don't have to apologize, Mark," she replied in a tired tone of voice. "You perceived me in a certain way and did what you thought you had to do." She hoped that he wouldn't notice that she still hurt.

"Actually, no, I didn't," Mark replied softly, coming closer to her. He slid his arms around her waist and pulled her to him, leaning his head over her. "I didn't think you were like my ex. It's just ingrained in me. That's something I used to do," he said with a shake of his head. "I stopped telling women who I was or what I was doing and kept them at arm-length," he explained, leaning his head on the top of hers. "I did the same thing with you. I know. It's just a bad habit that I didn't know how to break. That's all," he whispered in her hair.

Ella listened to him while absorbing his body's warmth. She had missed his touch during the last couple of days and longed to have him close to her. The young woman was happy that he had come to see her and was also content that he had the strength to say that he was sorry. She wouldn't have believed that Mark would apologize. Not when he did so well with flowers.

He nudged her head up with a finger under her chin and gazed into her eyes for a few moments. Then he whispered again, "I missed you, girl. Badly. And I missed us. We're good together. We've always had a good time together, Ella, haven't we?"

Ella hesitated for a moment but nodded. She stared into his troubled eyes, searching for answers to her questions.

Mark held her gaze, and then, his lips touched hers. He brushed his mouth to hers lightly, but both felt the warmth and the thrill of the feather-like touch. He merely sampled her warmth for a few moments, and only afterwards, he deepened his kiss, taking full possession of her mouth.

His hands slid along her back and traced every curve of her body. Ella shivered in his arms, and everything got back to normal in Mark's world.

Mark had been waiting for her complete surrender, and relief washed over him. Now, he knew that he hadn't lost Ella. She still belonged to him and with him.

His heart filled with joy, and his lips found the hollow between her neck and collarbone. His teeth scratched her skin, and she clung to his shoulders to keep her balance. She sighed, and her fingers burrowed in his coat. He raised his head and gazed into her eyes again. His lips curved upward. Ella was as lost in him as he was lost in her.

Mark would have loved nothing more but to drag Ella to bed and make love to her until morning. He had missed their physical connection. Still, the man knew that it would have been a wrong move. Moreover, he needed to reconnect with her, although he didn't understand that need.

Mark pulled back and let her go. His eyes swept around the room while searching for something to say. He noticed the shards on the floor, and his eyes widened. They covered every square foot around the TV area.

"New decorating style?" he asked, turning to her. His eyes sparkled with mischief.

Ella blushed, but then she shrugged. "I don't know why, but I always feel like throwing something at Colin." She looked over to what was left of another set of plates and shook her head. "I broke another set, damn it!"

Mark burst into laughter, tossing his head. "Whoa, I haven't seen this playful side of you so far. I think I like it as long as it's not aimed at me."

"Well," she replied dryly, glancing at him, "I've never felt the urge to break a plate over your head. Yet," she pointed out.

"And I can say that I'm very grateful for that. Let me help you pick up the shards," Mark offered.

"No, it isn't necessary. I've got a lot of practice doing that. Don't worry," she replied and went to take the broom and dustpan to clean the room. "Have a seat on the sofa until I finish," she invited him when she came back.

Obedient, Mark sat on the sofa and watched her clean the mess. Amusement brimmed in his eyes, and the corners of his mouth turned up. "What are you saying about going out for dinner? The Irish Pub down there," he nodded towards the direction of the pub.

"Yeah, why not?" she answered. "Let me get dressed. I need about five minutes."

"That I know. You're the only woman in my acquaintance who doesn't take forever to get ready to go out. If you say five minutes, then you're just five minutes."

Ella turned to him with a puzzled look on her face. "Is that what you want to talk about now? The women you know?"

"It was just a general observation, Ella. I'm not seeing anyone but you. I might have to take another woman for lunch, like my mom or one of my cousins. Not a date, though. Definitely, not a date," he shook his head, and his serious tone made her laugh.

"All right, don't try so hard. I believe you," Ella threw over her shoulder. Still laughing, she left the room.

Mark followed her by sight, trying to order his thoughts. He didn't know what was going on with him. He didn't need to insist that he wasn't dating any other woman. Both his words and muddled feelings for Ella made him vulnerable, and he didn't like that. He preferred to have control over his thoughts and actions.

CHAPTER FIFTEEN

FOUR DAYS BEFORE CHRISTMAS, Ella already felt excited. She had one week left of her vacation, so she took time off until January 6th. Ella didn't have any plans but needed time to unwind and think about where her life was going.

Her relationship with Mark was getting better and better every day.

Mark invited her to his office Christmas party and introduced her as his girlfriend. He even came to her company's party and made friends with everybody. People liked Mark and enjoyed talking to him. He was funny and easy-going if he wanted.

Many things surprised Ella about him. But he astonished her by asking about Mr. and Mrs. Thompson's divorce. Mark started having doubts about what his friend had told him and got mad, finding out the truth about that ugly divorce. His friend had lied, tracing a parallel between his marriage and Mark's failed engagement so that Mark would support him. Mark had ended that friendship without regrets. He couldn't trust that man anymore, and he never wasted time with people like that.

Mark impressed Ella more and more, and that spelled trouble. He stopped being just a pretty face, although he was devilishly handsome. Mark proved more profound than Ella had believed. Mark was kind in his casual way, although he showed some temper now and then. Yet, they matched each other there. Ella had one as well.

Mark had his flaws. Anyway, Ella knew that there wasn't such a thing as 'Mr. Right' out there. Maybe only someone who was almost right. A man like that would do for Ella.

Nevertheless, Ella didn't know how to make him understand that she was the right woman for him.

Although she didn't believe in fairy tales, Ella considered Christmas a magical period when everything was possible. She wanted to spend it with Mark.

Ella glanced at her watch. Mark would arrive at her office in a few minutes, so she put the files away and left her office.

That evening, she had to invite Mark for Christmas at her parents' house to make sure he didn't make other plans. On the other hand, Mark loved his freedom so much that he refused to define their relationship. Ella was afraid of his reaction and where their conversation might lead, and anxiety knotted her stomach.

Ella came out of the elevator, and her eyes fell on Mark. He didn't want her in danger again, so he had started waiting for her at the front desk. Now he was chatting with the security guard, and they seemed to have fun together.

Mark never thought that someone was beneath him, and Ella liked that. Even at her office Christmas party, his conversation made the stiffest lawyers lighten up and embrace the spirit of the party.

Mark sensed her presence and turned to her with a grin on his lips. He grinned like that if he had naughty plans for her in-store. Ella knew that grin very well, and she shivered.

She blushed and stopped a few steps away from him. Joy shone in Mark's eyes. He always enjoyed making her blush. He felt like ten feet tall. Mark strode to her lazily, his gaze fixed on her eyes, and he brushed his lips over hers.

They said goodnight to the security guard and left the lobby. Mark led Ella to his car, holding her arm so that she wouldn't slip on the wet pavement. It had snowed earlier, and as most of the time in Toronto, the snow melted almost immediately.

"You know what?" Mark turned to her after he started the car. "I think that this would be a great night to stay inside. Let's go to my place. Okay?"

Ella nodded, pleased with his proposition. Mark had invited her to his place only once before. She had never asked him for a repeat of that invitation afterwards. Ella preferred that they spent time in her apartment where she felt comfortable and confident, surrounded by her things.

However, Ella didn't understand why Mark had hesitated to invite her to his house. Situated in the north of the town, Mark's house didn't help anyone guess that the man was wealthy and didn't reveal anything about his personality or personal life.

The house wasn't opulent or flashy and looked like a comfortable roof over the head. Still, the giant fireplace in the living room made the room look romantic and brought some personality to the house. Mark didn't bother with the decor but created a functional habitat, where he slept and had breakfast in the morning.

Mark showed Ella inside and locked the door behind them. He went ahead to the living room, turning on the lights in his way.

"I'd like to go to the washroom and refresh a little if you don't mind," Ella said to him.

"I know you would," the man nodded, a finger trailing the length of her arm lazily.

Ella noticed that his eyes followed the finger and glimmered in the warm light from the corner lamp.

"If you want, you can even take a shower," he suddenly looked up at her. "I've noticed that a shower is the first thing on your list when you get home," he grinned at her impishly. "I've just bought your favourite shower gel, and you will find my bathrobe hanging on the door. You won't need anything else later, by the way," he whispered in her ear and kissed her before letting her go.

As always, her face flushed, and that made him grin. With a shake of her head, Ella left in a hurry. Still, she felt his eyes on her until she disappeared from the room.

ELLA CAME BACK, CLAD only in his bathrobe. She felt vulnerable in that skimpy attire, even though she doubted that her body held any secrets for Mark anymore. She found him putting the last touches on the dinner he had arranged on the round table from the breakfast nook.

The man had gone at long lengths with that dinner. He had ordered the food from one of his favourite restaurants, and Ella's mouth watered at the smell.

Mark invited her to sit down. Then he piled her plate with appetizers and filled her glass with red wine.

Stunned, Ella looked between him and the food, so Mark took a stuffed mushroom off the plate and brought it to her mouth. He waited until she opened her mouth and took it. Afterwards, he rubbed the corner of her mouth with his thumb. Mark leaned forward and kissed her, tasting her and the mushroom simultaneously.

When Mark pulled back, Ella chewed silently. Suddenly, she hungered for something other than the food on the table. Mark grinned devilishly at her as if he knew what she was thinking. He enjoyed the direction of her thoughts.

Mark started feeding her and himself at the same time as if she had forgotten to use a fork. After every bite, he would kiss her, lingering over her lips. Then his mouth started to err farther until it reached the back of her ear. The man licked the sensitive spot and then bit her earlobe suddenly, making her moan.

Mark didn't allow Ella to use her own hands, so dinner took a little more than usual. The man tormented her, alternating shallow kisses with deep ones and sucking at her lower lip or the skin of her neck. It felt downright decadent.

By the end of the dinner, Mark had aroused Ella thoroughly. All her senses heightened. She felt Mark's touches everywhere, and her belly quivered. She thought she would explode if he didn't take her to bed soon enough.

Mark finally finished with the food and stood, taking Ella's hand. He pulled her to him, and she practically screamed with relief.

Mark didn't take Ella to his bedroom. He pulled her down to the carpet in front of the fireplace, helping her to stretch on the floor. He opened her bathrobe and, fascinated, watched her pale skin in the light from the fire. Mark leaned and pulled her nipple into his mouth. Her blood sang, and she let herself go with the wave.

ELLA AND MARK SAT ON the floor, leaning on the sofa and drinking wine. Although Ella's body had just exploded in hundreds of stars, Mark's words still aroused her. Mark said that he hadn't finished making love to her yet, so they didn't bother to get dressed.

Content and happy, Mark played with her fingers and kissed them, now and then. His happiness brought warm and fuzzy feelings to Ella's heart.

She waited for a while until she thought it was the right time to talk to him. Anyway, she couldn't think of any other better moment.

"Mark," she started hesitantly, and his gaze turned to her face as if he felt her uncertainty.

"Yes, Ella. What is it?" he asked softly.

"I wanted to ask you something," Ella said but stopped immediately, almost regretting that she had started talking.

Mark squeezed her hand encouragingly. "Come on, baby. It can't be so bad. Just ask."

"Well, I wouldn't want to give you any wrong ideas," she said, stealing a glance at him and then turning her eyes back to her glass. "I'd like you to come and spend Christmas with me," she finally said and waited for his answer, feeling her heart in her boots.

Mark didn't answer immediately, though. He looked at her, and she could see that he somehow felt sorry for her, knowing that he would refuse her demand.

"You're going to your parents' house, Ella, aren't you?" Mark asked her.

"Yes, I am," she answered, keeping her head down. She couldn't look at him.

"Okay, enough of that," Mark said. He put his glass down and turned her head to him with his thumb. Ella couldn't do anything else but look at him now.

"Ella, I can't ask you not to go to your parents for Christmas. I know you've always been doing that. I understand very well it's a tradition for your family, and they're waiting for you. Yet, I can't come with you. I'm not ready for the meeting the parents part now. Honestly, I don't know if I'll ever be. I hope you understand. I've always been upfront with what you can expect from me."

Ella didn't answer, but he could see that she was hurt. Mark would have spared her, but he had promised himself never to lie to her, so he had to be brutally honest no matter what.

"Ella..." he started, but she put her hand up and stopped him.

"No, Mark, I understand. You've never implied that things would be different someday, and I should have known better than asking you to do that," she replied and tried to stand up.

"You're upset," Mark said, rising off the floor and helping her stand, as well.

"No, no, no, I'm not upset with you," Ella shook her head. "I don't know. I knew that you wouldn't do forever or anything like that. But ... it's Christmas, you know. And I wanted to be with you," she explained in a sad tone of voice. "Now, look at me. I ruined our evening together," she continued and turned her head away when tears welled in her eyes.

Mark didn't let her hide her face and turned her back to him. He leaned in and kissed her. His kiss wasn't his usual kiss, full of heat. It was a kiss to comfort. It overwhelmed her, and a tear fell on her cheek. Mark wiped it with his thumb and then took her head in his hands.

"Look, baby, I know. But let's do this. You go and spend some time with your family, and when you're back, you'll have all the time you want with me, all right?"

Ella read determination in his eyes, and she understood that he meant what he said. She nodded and then looked at their glasses on the floor. She didn't know what to do.

"I think I should go," she said, but he shook his head.

"Come on, Ella. It's two more days until you have to leave. Why don't we spend these days together?" Mark asked her.

"Well, tomorrow I should go and buy some presents for my family... Every year, I promise to start shopping early, and every year, I must hurry and do the shopping at the last minute. So..."

"All right, Ella, it's not a problem. Then, it's decided. We'll go shopping tomorrow. After we finish shopping, we can spend the rest of the evening and the night together, baby. And you'll be back on 26th, I think."

She nodded but then corrected herself. "Actually, I might be staying until the 27th, I don't know. It depends on how crazy my mom can make me by then," Ella admitted morosely.

"All right, then. But you have my number, and you can call me at any hour, day or night. I'll see my parents on Christmas Eve, as always, but I'll have my phone with me. If things get worse, call me," Mark ordered in a tone that didn't broach any refusal. Ella smiled at him and nodded. Then, on tiptoe, she kissed the corner of his mouth. "Now, come on, we have to try round two," he said and pulled her back on the floor with him.

CHAPTER SIXTEEN

ELLA DROVE INTO WHITBY before eight. She felt restless, so she left home the first thing that morning.

She missed Mark's body next to hers and spent a terrible night. The man decided to let her rest before her trip and left early the previous evening.

Ella regretted that she hadn't left soon after Mark's departure, even though she would have arrived at her parents' house around eleven or midnight. Her parents didn't go to bed early, so her arrival wouldn't have been a problem. At least, she might have felt less edgy in their company, and part of her sadness might have vanished.

Ella parked in her parents' driveway at eight-fifteen and opened the trunk. Her eyes fell on the pile of things inside, and with a sigh, she started gathering them. Ella had received a long list from her mother. She had to bring many things from Toronto besides the gifts she had bought.

Steps came from behind her, and she turned. Her eyes fell on her father, who was coming towards her with a big smile on his face.

"Hello, there, pussycat, long time, eh?" he said and took her in his arms, holding her tight.

That astonished her. Her father had never shown too much emotion, and he had always acted as if it hadn't been a big deal when she came to visit them.

It was true that this time Ella hadn't had the time to visit her family for almost half a year, even though the distance wasn't so great. Yet, she'd never imagined that her father would have missed her so much.

After giving her another squeeze, he kissed her cheek again. Then he pushed her at an arm-length and took a good look at her.

"Well, you look tired, but I expected that. I know you work long hours, and you woke up quite early today. Otherwise, you look good, Ella. Come on. I'll help you carry all of those. What did you do? Emptied all the shops in Toronto?" he asked and chuckled, making her smile.

"Hardly, dad. I've just brought a few presents. Ah, and that stuff mom asked me to buy."

"Ah, the stuff she asked you to buy. I see," her father said and started collecting bags as well.

They went inside, and all the way, he asked Ella all sorts of questions about her work and life, taking care not to touch on too personal matters. Ella answered as well as she could. She was satisfied that he showed some interest in her life, even if he asked generic questions.

Once inside, they put the gifts under the tree. Then, Ella's father led the way to the kitchen where her mother worked.

"Oh, Ella, you're here," she exclaimed. She wiped her hands on her apron and hurried to hug her daughter.

"Hi, mom," Ella managed to say while her mother smothered her with hugs and kisses.

"Well, let me look at you," her mother asked, taking a step back. "You know, you can stand to lose a few pounds. I don't think that young man of yours would mind it," she said reproachfully. "And by the way, where's he? I really love him, you know. You're so lucky you landed a doctor, Ella. I've never thought you could," she continued to talk like a magpie.

"Mother," Ella said in a steely tone of voice. "First of all, he's not my nice man. I've already told you that I broke up with him, and that's it."

"Oh, no, that's stupid of you, Ella," her mother hastened to reply. "He's meant for you. Look, go and call him immediately. Invite him here. It's the best thing you could do. Listen to me, I'm your mother, and I know what I'm talking about."

"No, mother, I won't call him. Not now and not ever. First, he cheated on me..." she started to say, but her mother waved her concern away.

"Don't be so prissy, Ella. Men have...their needs," she said.

"What about me?" her father intervened in a stern voice, and both women looked at him nonplussed. They hadn't noticed that he was still standing there.

Ella was also surprised because her father had never cared about what her mother said to her before. She couldn't believe that he took a stand for her, his face cut in stone.

His question didn't sit very well with her. His attitude dumbfounded her mother as well. "What about you?" the woman finally asked.

"If men have... How did you put it? Oh, yeah, needs. Then I also can cheat on you without regrets or fear that my actions would lead to later discussions between us," Ella's pointed out.

"Don't be absurd," his wife answered diffidently, waving her hand. "It's not the same thing, and you know it."

"How isn't it the same?" he insisted, not ready to let the subject go. "You said that it didn't matter if Colin cheated on Ella. He had needs. That means that I can also cheat on you if I have needs, and you should accept my behaviour without complaints."

Ella clenched her fists wryly. She didn't know what to believe anymore. She knew that her father wouldn't cheat on her mother, but something didn't seem right with what he said.

"Honey," her mother replied to him, "we are married, the two of us. Of course, Colin won't cheat on her when they're married."

"Are you sure?" her father replied in a crisp tone of voice. "Are you sure he won't? I know that he is a cheat. A man like that cheats before marriage and afterwards. There's no cure for that, especially if he knows that it's allowed."

"All right, all right," Ella's mother snapped. "But look at her," she waved her hand in Ella's direction. "She's alone. She's old. She's got too many pounds on. Ella has to take what she can. She doesn't have too many chances left."

Her father just looked at his wife for a few moments, shook his head in disbelief, and then turned to Ella. "Listen, pumpkin, you might be alone right now, but your life isn't over yet. You've got enough time left, and someone's out there for you. You don't have to settle for that prick. You're not old yet. Not even at half of your life. And your pounds look just fine. Don't worry about it, okay?"

Ella's eyes swam with tears. Not only had she never expected her father to be on her side, but she had never imagined that he would tell her such things. She hugged him tightly, even if he fidgeted a little, feeling embarrassed.

"Thank you, daddy. And don't worry. I won't settle for Colin. He also hit me, so... I'm sorry, mother," Ella said, turning to her mother. The woman stared at her daughter with shock-stricken wide eyes. "I won't call him, and I won't ever talk to him. Even if he were the last man left on earth."

"What do you mean he hit you?" her father roared when he finally processed her words.

"Yes, how did he hit you?" her mother echoed her husband's words.

"Well, he came to my house after he spoke to you," she explained to her mother. "He didn't like hearing that I didn't want to get back in a relationship with him."

"I'm going to dismember him! I'll rip his limbs off! One by one!" her father shouted and started to the door, ready to drive to Toronto and find the prick who had hurt his little girl.

"Dad," Ella blocked his path. "You don't need to do that. He got what he deserved," she continued and nodded to emphasize her words.

"Don't tell me you beat him," her mother asked bitterly. "I don't believe that you could beat him. Let your father go...."

"Mom," Ella interrupted her. "Of course, I couldn't, but Mark could."

"Who the heck is Mark?" her father asked with exasperation.

Her mother looked as if she stretched her ears, so she wouldn't miss a word. Her face was so comical that Ella had difficulty not bursting into laughter.

"Mark is my boyfriend," she replied. "He's a big guy, and if you want to know, he scared Colin so bad that he wet his pants."

Both her parents looked at Ella as if they couldn't believe it. Then, her father burst into gales of laughter.

"He did? Did he pee in his pants? Really?"

"Yes, dad, he did. So, you don't need to go and teach him a lesson. Mark had already taught Colin that. Okay?"

"And where's this Prince Charming?" her father asked Ella.

"Sorry?" she replied.

Ella knew what he wanted to know. However, she needed time to think of something to say.

"This Mark," he repeated. "Your knight. Where is he? Why isn't he here with you?" her father insisted.

She hesitated for a few moments, but she had to answer because both her parents were waiting. She knew that they wouldn't let it go.

"Well, he's in Toronto. He had something to do, and...All right, he's not ready to meet you two. Okay? That's it. Now you know," Ella told them the truth.

Neither her mother nor her father answered. Both were merely looking at her. After a couple of minutes, her father came forward and put his hand on her shoulder.

"Listen, honey. Does Mark treat you well? Are you happy with him?"

Ella nodded. Mark might have been afraid of a monogamous relationship. Still, despite his fears, he treated her well, and she was happy with him.

"Well, then everything's fine, Ella. And I won't go after that excuse of a man if Mark had already beat me to the punch," her father said, smiling, and left the kitchen.

Once he left, her mother came to Ella and pulled her to the kitchen table.

"Sit here and tell me everything about him. After that, go and call him. Ask him to come here," Ella's mother demanded.

"Mom, I can tell you about him, but I won't ask him to come here. You have to understand that this isn't negotiable," Ella said in an implacable tone of voice. Her mother looked like she wanted to argue her point.

CHAPTER SEVENTEEN

ELLA HAD ALREADY LEFT, and Mark felt at odds. He had spent most of his time with her lately, and now he felt deserted. He didn't know what to do with his time.

Walking the streets without purpose, he stopped at a known watering hole for a drink. It was so freezing outside that his nose felt like an icicle. He needed a glass of whiskey to get back on track and continue his restless stroll.

Mark sat on a barstool at the bar and signalled the bartender.

"We haven't seen you around for quite a while," the man said. "The usual?"

"Yes, please," Mark replied. "I was busy elsewhere," he answered the bartender's masked question.

"I see. Well, this is a good night for a single malt," the bartender replied with a wink for Mark.

He turned and took a bottle off the shelf behind him. He showed Mark the bottle, and the man nodded. The bartender poured some whiskey for Mark, put the bottle back on the shelf and took a cloth to wipe the counter. He opened his mouth to continue the conversation with Mark when a gorgeous young woman came to the bar. The man forgot everything about Mark and hastened at her.

"What can I get you?" he asked, and his smile got wider.

The woman didn't smile back but replied, "The same as him."

Her answer made Mark turn to her. She noticed the recognition and shocking surprise in Mark's eyes.

"Hello, Jo. Jo, isn't it?" he said, trying to appear nonchalant. However, the woman knew men and how they reacted.

"Well, at least you have a good memory," she replied in a glacial voice.

"So, what brings you in my part of the woods?" Mark asked. "Something tells me this is not one of your usual hangouts."

His voice was dripping with sarcasm, but Jo didn't seem to care. She was the same ice woman he remembered from the night when he met Ella.

"That's none of your business," she replied and then sipped from her glass.

"Well, princess, then move on to better pastures. I'm not interested in entertaining a cold and frigid maiden."

Mark knew he was mean, but he had his own black thoughts and didn't feel like dealing with Jo right then. He had already been missing Ella, and Jo's presence deepened his longing.

"I'm not so impressionable, and I don't scare easy," the woman replied, using a tone of voice appropriate to an inferior creature.

Her words made Mark grit his teeth, and his eyes glinted.

"Nevertheless, I care about Ella," Jo continued. "We might have some disagreements sometimes, but Ella's a good person. She's one of the truly good people. And you broke her heart with your selfishness," she said with heat in her voice. Anger blazed in the woman's eyes, and Mark stared at her, fascinated.

He shook his head to clear it and then replied, "I haven't broken her heart. You should get your facts right," he lectured, but she stopped him, putting up her hand.

"It's Christmas tomorrow. You're here. She's there, in Whitby," Jo replied, tossing her head. "I know Ella, and I say that you broke her heart. That's not something I'd forget. I can be a nasty enemy, one you shouldn't have made."

"Come on, I don't care about that," he shot back at her. "But why do you think I broke her heart? Just because I didn't go with her there for Christmas?"

"Yes, Sherlock. You guessed. Christmas is the most important time of the year for her. It embodies love, understanding, and happiness in Ella's mind. With you here, she can't be happy, especially with that overbearing mother of hers. That woman would take cheap shots at her for being alone and make her feel unworthy. She'd push Ella back to Colin, and that I can't accept," Jo shook her head in anger.

"Her own mother? Would push her back to the man who hit her?" Mark wondered with incredulity.

"He hit her?" she cried out. "The creep hit her? When the heck did that happen?"

"Well, some time ago, so don't sweat it. I took care of Colin."

"Well, at least you were good at something," she shot over her shoulder, leaving the bar.

Mark's eyes followed her. The woman went to a table with about ten or twelve people. He shook his head to clear it and turned back to his drink.

He gazed at his watch and wondered what Ella was doing right then. Was she baking cookies or singing carols?

Mark missed her. It was just the second day without her, and the thought that he had to wait at least two more days to see her drove him out of his mind.

His mother was waiting for him to come to dinner, but he didn't feel like eating right then. He felt like drinking until he would crash into his bed without thinking of Ella anymore.

Then, it hit him. He wasn't afraid of what Ella would do to him. He was scared that he might not have his forever with her, and that was plain stupid. She had already offered him that, and he had pushed her away.

Thinking of what Jo had said, that Christmas was the most crucial time for Ella, Mark knew what he had to do.

CHAPTER EIGHTEEN

ELLA TALKED TO HER grandmother for a couple of hours already, and the woman baffled her. It was after eleven, and she still had enough stamina to reminiscence.

She told Ella stories about the Christmases they spent together when Ella was little. The woman could recall every prank Ella had ever played on her sister and brother.

That year, only Ella's brother had come with his wife for holidays. His sons had gone abroad with a group of friends, and Ella's sister had gone away with her family.

As usual, Ella's father watched a game on TV with her brother. Her mother brought him another beer and a pitcher of eggnog for the women to share.

She filled granny's glass first, and then she poured eggnog in Ella's. Marge, her daughter-in-law, refused, saying that she had had enough for one evening. She preferred beer, but she didn't want to hurt her mother-in-law's feelings.

The guys were bellowing at the TV when knocks sounded at the front door. They all looked at each other with bewilderment. They couldn't imagine who would come for a visit at that hour on Christmas Eve.

Ella's mother stood up to go and answer, but her father waved her to sit back and went to the front door. He looked through the glass of the door to see who had knocked. However, he didn't recognize the man on the steps.

Nevertheless, he opened the door. He didn't believe that such a well-dressed man would have come to rob them on Christmas Eve.

"Yes?" he asked.

"Hello, I'm Mark. I know it's late, but may I speak to Ella, please?"

Eager to hear what was going on at the door, everybody in the living room kept quiet. Ella's brother had muted the TV, so Ella overheard Mark's voice very clear. She stood up, only to discover that her legs shook.

She couldn't imagine what brought Mark there or how he knew to get there. He didn't have her parents' address from her.

Ella went to the front door, and her father stepped aside, whispering to her, "It's your White Knight, Ella." Then he left, leaving her alone with Mark.

Ella wanted to say something, but her mouth couldn't form any words, and her brain went blank. She had Mark before her eyes, and she had no explanation for his presence.

"Ella," Mark came to her and pulled her to his chest in a tight hug. Then, he whispered to her, "I couldn't be without you. Not even two days, and I was going silently mad. I need you in my life. As you said, forever."

Mark pulled back at an arm's length. However, he didn't let go of Ella. He tried to read the woman's thoughts on her face but noticed that Ella's eyes shone with unshed tears.

"I hope you won't cry now, Ella. I didn't think that you'd get upset because I tracked you here," he said, his voice less confident than usual.

"Don't be silly, Mark. Of course, I'm not upset that you're here. Why would I be? I wanted you here. But how did you know where to come?" Ella inquired with bafflement.

"I asked Jo," Mark replied. Noticing her surprise, he waved his hand. "It's a long story. Believe me. And it doesn't really matter. By the way, I just asked you to marry me, and you said nothing," he said reproachfully.

"You did? I haven't heard that. Something must be wrong with my ears," she replied, patting her right ear.

"Come on, don't be mean... I said forever, didn't I?" Mark said, stroking her face.

"Ah, and does that mean that you're asking me to marry you?" Ella wondered in a teasing tone of voice.

"You're a smart girl, Ella. You know to read between the lines. Come on, it might not be the most romantic proposal, but I did ask you to be my wife."

"But..."

"Oh, damn it," he interrupted her. "Okay, I see that you want me to say the words. I will. Will you be my wife?"

Ella hardly kept her laughter contained. Mark's voice sounded very angry. She was sure that no one had ever received such a furious marriage proposal.

"All right, Mark, I will. You don't have to snap at me."

Now Ella let her laughter fly free, but Mark stopped it with a bruising kiss. Exclamations erupted behind her, and she had one second to realize that her family had heard Mark's words before she forgot about everything.

When Mark raised his head, Ella's body already hummed. Her heart recognized the perfect mate in Mark. The man shoved his hand in his pocket and took out an old little box. He lifted the lid of the box, revealing a vintage engagement ring.

"My grandmother left the ring to me. And don't worry, Ella. No one has worn this ring beside her," Mark said and slid the engagement ring on Ella's finger.

Ella gazed at the ring. Then she looked up at Mark, and tears of happiness fell on her cheek. Her Christmas wish had come true.

AUTHOR'S BIOGRAPHY

ROWENA DAWN writes romance, reads thrillers and watches comedies. She likes walking through the woods but insanely loves the sea. She has a love - hate relationship with her writing and drives her dog crazy whenever she doesn't stop writing to take him out. And yes, she bakes, bread and cakes. Apparently good ones - they're always in demand.

ALSO BY ROWENA DAWN

LEAP OF FAITH
Double-Edged – Book One in The Perfect Halves Series
Eyes in the Dark – Book Two in The Perfect Halves Series
Pulled In – Book Three in The Perfect Halves Series
Becka's Awakening – Book One in The Winstons Series
Matt's Dilemma – Book Two in The Winstons Series
Jay's Salvation – Book Three in The Winstons Series
Catching Lily – Live Wire – Book Four in The Perfect Halves Series & The Winstons Series
Ariel's Redemption – Book Five in The Winstons Series
Forthcoming:
Alex's Wake Up Call - Book Six in The Winstons Series

If you enjoyed this book, please, leave a review. There's no more joy for an author than to see their work is read and enjoyed.

Thank you.

Rowena Dawn

Did you love *Mr. (Almost) Right*? Then you should read *Becka's Awakening*[1] by Rowena Dawn!

[2]

Becka wanted the power and the money. What she got was losing her heart.

Becka is a witch and not a very good one. With her great-grandmother's curse hanging over her she has no idea how to escape her fate. When she suddenly spills her coffee on a stranger she finds out there's more to life than what she thought. But is she ready for what that means?

---

1. https://books2read.com/u/bPJD2A

2. https://books2read.com/u/bPJD2A

Becka's Awakening is the first book in Rowena Dawn's The Winstons Series. If you like paranormal romance, then you'll love a series that features compelling characters.

Buy this paranormal romance filled with sensuous heat today!

About the Publisher

It is based in Toronto and brings to public various books: poems, novels, short-stories, children's books, language study books and non-fiction. It publishes the literary review: Scarlet Leaf Review: www.scarletleafreview.com

Our mission is to help emerging authors and poets to make their works known to the public.

Contact email address: scarletleafpublishinghouse@gmail.com